LUCKY BY MAGIC

LOST BY MAGIC: BOOK 2

DAVID NETH

DN Publishing

Lucky by Magic
Lost by Magic, Book 2
Copyright © 2023 by David Neth
Batavia, NY

www.DavidNethBooks.com

ISBN: 978-1-945336-45-4
First Edition

Subscribe to the author's newsletter for updates and exclusive content:
DavidNethBooks.com/Newsletter

Follow the author at:
www.facebook.com/DavidNethBooks

Also by David Neth

Lost by Magic
Lost by Magic
Lucky by Magic
Lured by Magic

Coven
Harpy
Siren
Valkyrie
Shapeshifter
Sorcerer
Witch (Short Story)
Enchantress
Oracle
Trickster
Poltergeist
Hex (Short Story)
Witch Hunter
Demon (Short Story)

Under the Moon
The Full Moon
The Harvest Moon
The Blood Moon
The Crescent Moon
The Blue Moon

The Art of Magic

Fuse
Origin
Omertà
Oblivion

Heat
Black Magnet
Dust Storm
The Gatekeeper

Standalone
All I Ever Wanted

Suicide Hotline

If you or a loved one is considering suicide, please utilize the following resources:

Call/Text: 988 (in the U.S.)
Visit online: https://988lifeline.org/

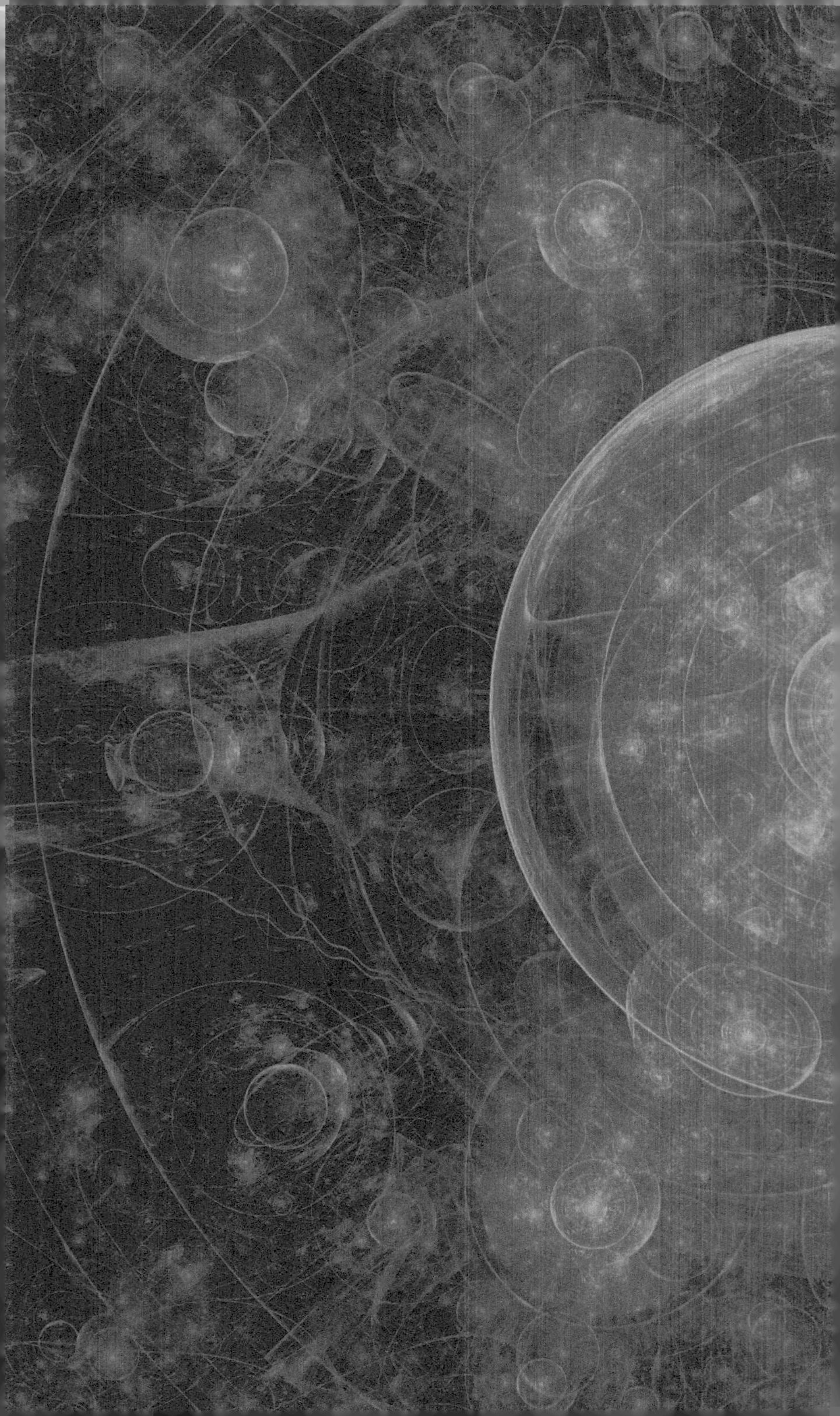

CHAPTER 1

"Read 'em and weep, boys!" Charles Bennett laid out his cards on the table, much to the dismay of his poker buddies. Another Royal Flush. He had won the last three games with the same hand. The cards seemed to find a way into his possession, no matter how well the deck was shuffled or who dealt.

"That's it." Tony tossed his cards in the air and leaned back in his chair. "I swear, you have to be cheating somehow."

"And where would I be hiding the cards?" Charles sat with his suit jacket off and his shirtsleeves rolled up to his elbows, which his buddies had insisted on after the second game he won.

Jeffrey shook his head. "If he's playing again, I'm done. I need to keep the little money I have left!"

Charles collected the pile of dollar bills on the table and began sorting them into stacks. This was his third night playing at the Erie Club, and every game he played, he won. By a significant amount each time.

"All right, boys," Charles said with a grin. "I'll even the score and head on home. It's getting late and the missus is going to want me there, if you catch my drift." He waved his cigar and gave a wink.

"Just take your money and go," Robert told him.

"*Our* money," Tony corrected.

Charles finished collecting the cash up, then slipped it in his suit coat pocket. He rose and pulled the jacket on. What had started out as a friendly weekly game turned into a tension-filled glutton show, and Charles was the only one smiling.

Of course, Charles didn't care. As long as he was the one winning, that was all that mattered.

When Charles finally made it onto West 6th Street, his driver was already waiting for him at the curb.

The ride home was short. In truth, it would've been just as easy to walk, but being that it was just after midnight and, more importantly, that Charles simply had the money to waste, he opted for the driver.

The Bennett house was among the many grand brick

homes on West 6ᵗʰ between Myrtle and Chestnut. It was another status symbol for the neighborhood to see. One that he spent a fortune on, simply because of the address.

Inside, Charles went right to the credenza where he and his wife, Catherine, kept the liquor in the front den — ready for any guests who may arrive — and poured himself a glass of bourbon. Even though alcohol was technically outlawed, Charles found that rules of that nature didn't always extend to the people of his class. That is, unless they were a part of the temperance movement. But those people made themselves known, so Charles was careful around them.

Taking a seat in the sitting room, Charles set his glass on the table beside his usual chair and reached over to click on the lamp. When the light illuminated the room, however, he was stunned to see a woman sitting in the chair opposite him.

Not just any woman. *Her.*

She was as beautiful as he remembered. Her long blonde hair was draped over one shoulder. She wore a white hat with a thin rim that held a short veil to cover her eyes. Her dress was white and hugged her body tighter than Charles was used to seeing on a woman.

At the sight of her, Charles could feel his heart begin to race. She always had a way of making him flustered.

"Charles," she said with a sneer.

Lucky by Magic

Stunned, he couldn't speak.

The woman rose to her feet and walked around the room. "You've done quite well for yourself, haven't you?" Her fingers traced over the ornate furniture, which had been hand-crafted by a fine carpenter and upholstered with fabric of his wife's choosing.

"I dare say, you are one of my most successful clients," she went on. "And to think that you've accomplished all of this in just a year. My, how your life has changed."

"I would've gotten all of this eventually."

The woman slapped both hands against the back of the chair she stood behind. "Wrong!" she bellowed. "You had *nothing*. Otherwise, you wouldn't have called on me."

"Keep your voice down," he warned through gritted teeth. "I don't want my wife to hear you."

"You mean the one you married only because your luck changed? Your fortune isn't the only thing that came from me. I gave you a job, fame, even that beautiful woman waiting for you upstairs. And now I've come to collect on the debt that you owe me."

Charles shook his head, tears welling in his eyes. "Please. Don't hurt her."

The woman let out a forced laugh. "Ha! Like I give a damn about her. No, you are the one with a debt to settle, so you are the one who needs to pay." She gestured around the room. "Get ready to kiss all of this goodbye."

The rich man dropped to his knees and scampered across the room. "Please, no! I need a little more time! You can't just take all of this away from me!"

"These were the terms you agreed to, Mr. Bennett. You knew all along that this day was coming. What's done is done."

Charles moved around the chair and wrapped his arms around her legs, desperate. "I'll do anything! Just don't take this away!"

Placing a hand on his forehead, she pushed him away as she stepped out of his locked arms. "Don't be so pathetic, Mr. Bennett. This visit was merely a courtesy call to tell you that the deal has expired." She started to the door. "Your payment won't be collected right away. But it won't be long."

"When will it start?" There was defeat in his tone.

"Your fall will be much like your rise. Quick." From behind her veil, she winked at him. "Good luck, Mr. Bennett." She exited through the front door, laughing to herself.

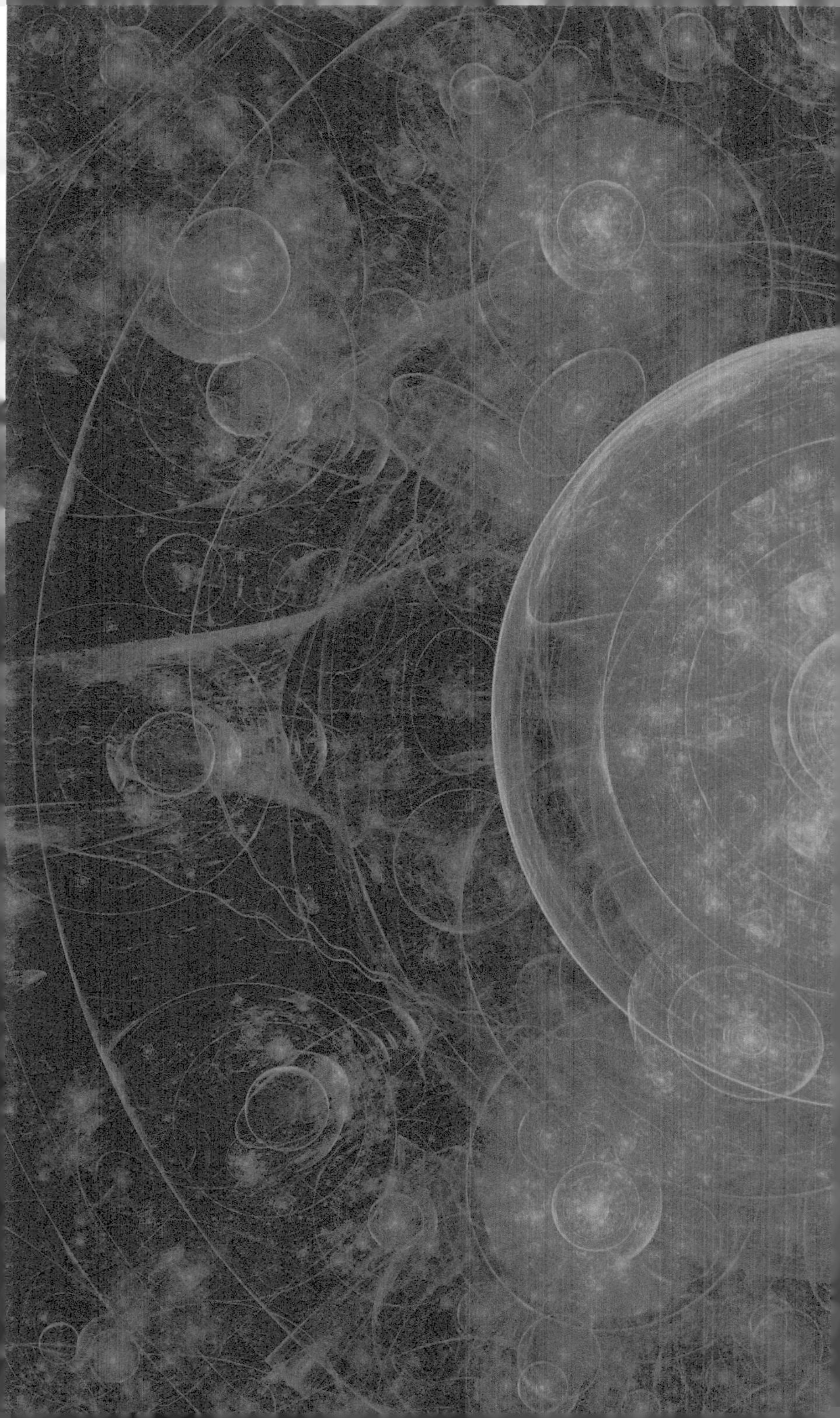

CHAPTER 2

Frankie turned left from Peach Street onto Cherry south of the city line. In 1984, this area would be dominated by wide-lanes roads, oversized parking lots, gas stations, and drive-thrus. In 1924, however, it was dirt roads following the city's street grid, with many houses still under construction. Houses that, in Frankie's time, would be torn down for a commercial venture of some sort.

He walked by Glenwood Park, which extended to Cherry Street. In his time, there was a large golf course between Cherry and Glenwood Park. So to see it extending much further was disorienting. Everything was similar to what he remembered, but also so different.

Lucky by Magic

He couldn't help but wonder if the Erie that he remembered from 1984 was the vision of a future Erie that residents in the 20s saw for their city.

On Arlington, Frankie looked around in awe as the grand houses he'd always admired growing up were still under construction. Many of the large trees that so beautifully shaded his street were still tiny saplings, or not even planted at all. There were no sidewalks or driveways. Dirt and dust wafted through the air from the gravel road that had yet to be paved.

Frankie made his way down the street, which became more wild and natural with vegetation the farther from Cherry Street he got. Again, it amazed him to see how the city had been carved out of the natural landscape. Beyond Arlington, south of the city, were remnants of farmland that were likely already slated for development.

Frankie took a seat on the grass across from his house. There were a few mature trees that sat back away from the street, although the street-lining trees that he remembered were nowhere in sight yet.

His home looked generally the same. There were some finer architectural details missing—window dressings, stained glass, landscaping. The biggest missing piece was the kitchen addition to the left of the house. Idly, Frankie wondered where the kitchen was in this current house, since the addition had been a part of the house for as long as he could remember.

There was a single car parked in the gravel driveway. It matched all the other cars Frankie had seen from this time period: cloth roof, thin glass, sidestep panels that covered the tops of the wheels. Being that Arlington was a relatively remote area in the 20s, a car would be necessary. Still, it surprised him. His grandfather was a woodworker and his grandmother was a homemaker until her early death. From what he remembered from the stories his father had told him, luxuries such as cars weren't something his grandfather would've indulged in. Then again, the trolley line only came as far as 26th Street. A car would be important.

Frankie thought more about the dates. His father, James, was born in November 1924, which would mean that Frankie's grandmother, Anna, would be pregnant with him now. Maybe he could go in and talk to Anna and—

"Frankie!"

The force of the cry drew his attention more than the call of his name did.

Evelyn marched down the road before stopping in front of him and crossing her arms. "What *on earth* do you think you're doing?"

"I—"

Lucky by Magic

"If you exposed yourself to your family, you could've severely altered the timeline and *your existence* could've been erased and then we'd all be stuck in a strange time loop because if you changed things to the point where you never come back here, then you wouldn't have been able to make the changes that altered the future."

Frankie narrowed his eyes, confused at what exactly she had just said. "I haven't gone in. I've just been thinking."

Evelyn studied him, then let out a sigh and took a seat beside him. "About what?"

He shrugged in response and kept his eyes on the house.

"Is that the house you lived in before you came back to our time?" she asked.

He nodded. "Grew up right here. In my time, it's a little more put together." He pointed. "Over there, there's an addition that gets put on in the 40s, I think. The whole yard is landscaped really nicely. The color is basically the same, but it's more decorative. The trim and colors and everything is a little more elegant. Makes us look like we have more money than we do."

"*Did* you have a lot of money at one point? I mean, your family."

He shook his head. "Not really. We've always been comfortable. My grandfather was a carpenter—or is right now, I guess. In this time. He spent a lot of time adding different details to the house. It started as a simple ten-by-ten box that really just served the family on their farm. It had been added to and built up over generations. My grandfather is the one who really took it up a notch."

Evelyn smiled, but didn't say anything else.

After a moment, Frankie said, "I came back to get my hands on our family magic book. I was hoping to find a spell or a ritual or *something* to return me back to my time."

"But going back and interacting with your family could be dangerous," Evelyn warned.

"I know. And that's why I haven't gone in yet."

Evelyn put her hand on his back.

"It's just frustrating that the answer could be *right there* and I can't get to it." He wiped his hands in his pants. Wool. Time-period appropriate. Very formal. And very itchy. Evelyn and Levi had gotten him some clothes so he could blend in better. He still missed his regular clothes. Just like he missed his own time period.

And his girls.

Evelyn rubbed his back. "We'll find a way."

Frankie could tell she was just saying that to make him feel better. As an oracle, if she truly knew how he could get back to his time, she would tell him. Even help him accomplish it. The fact that she only offered words of encouragement told him that she didn't know any more than he did.

The front door of the house opened and both Frankie and Evelyn got to their feet and tried not to draw attention to themselves. However, the woman who exited looked completely unfamiliar to Frankie. She was blonde, with her hair draped over one shoulder, and a rimmed hat that held a short veil over her eyes. She wore a white fitted dress and heels, which seemed to be in complete contrast to the dust and noise coming from the end of the street.

"Is that your grandmother?" Evelyn whispered. "She's beautiful."

"No, it's not," he said. "I have no idea who she is."

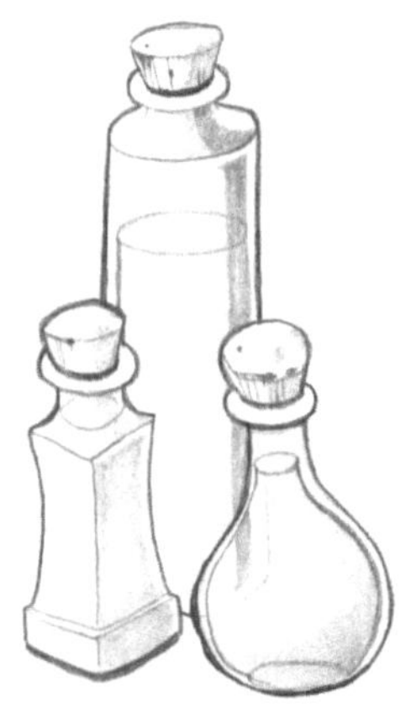

CHAPTER 3

The lunch break was much needed. Not only for the girls, but for Marie and her in-laws as well. After taking the girls' orders, then hearing the many changes that came while she waited in line, Marie was happy that James and Helen, her husband's parents, had agreed to take Samantha and Kathy to find a table among all of the other zoo visitors taking a mid-day break.

By the time Marie arrived with the food, she could tell that her youngest, Kathy, who had just turned three, was on the verge of a meltdown. There would certainly be a nap somewhere in her near future.

"Here, let me cut that up for you," James leaned over

and used his plastic silverware to cut up Samantha's burger into smaller pieces.

Helen, meanwhile, hovered over Kathy and picked up the various pieces of food that continued to fall onto the ground.

"Are you girls having fun?" Marie asked in between bites of her own burger. The lunch options were limited—and expensive.

"Yeah!" Kathy cheered.

"What was your favorite part?" Helen asked.

"The lions!"

Marie smiled. "I liked them too. What about you, Sam?"

Her older daughter thought about it a moment. "Hmm. I think the orangutans."

"Are we going to stay here all day?" Kathy tried to maneuver her hand to her mouth to lick up the ketchup she had splattered on herself. When she opened her mouth to lick it off, chewed pieces of food fell out of her mouth.

"Here, let Grandma get that for you." Helen chased after Kathy with a napkin. Kathy, however, whined and swatted her grandmother away.

"We'll have time to see everything else," Marie answered. "There isn't much left, we've seen most of it. Is there anything you want to see again?"

Both girls shook their head.

"What do you say we go back home and play in the yard with the hose?"

The girls cheered.

Summer was definitely gearing up. The forecast said it could reach just over 70 degrees and Marie was anxious to get the girls home and rested before the heat really set in. So far, though, it had been a gorgeous day. And it wasn't too crowded, being that school was still in session, which lessened the crowd.

Marie crumpled up the wrapper from her meal and gathered some of the other trash they had collected since they sat down. Leaning over to James, she said, "I'm going to run to the bathroom real quick. You mind keeping an eye on them?"

He smiled and waved her on. "They're fine. Take your time."

Marie left the table and went in search of the bathrooms. Signs pointed to just around the corner, but a blood-curdling scream stopped her in her tracks. It was coming from the jaguar exhibit.

She took off in a run, following the source of the scream.

Inside, the first thing she saw was a child cowering in the corner. He was sitting on the floor with his knees tucked up against him and his arms covering his face.

Lucky by Magic

Marie's first thought was that he was afraid of the jaguar, but one look inside the pen told her that couldn't be the case. The jaguar was sleeping on the opposite side. It barely lifted its head to even look at the crying child.

The other thought that struck her was where this boy's parents could be. She began to walk toward him to console him, but stopped when she saw a woman in the shadows.

But something was off about her. Not only was her hair gray and matted and her back was just a little hunched over, but the way she kneaded her knotted hands as she stared blankly at the boy with glassy eyes didn't sit well with Marie.

"What are you doing to him?" the witch demanded of the woman.

As soon as the woman's focus shifted to Marie, the boy stopped crying instantly.

The woman's eyes were mesmerizing. So focused and yet so strange. Too defined. As if they weren't quite natural.

After a second, she darted toward the entrance.

"Hey!" Marie called to her. Before the woman could reach the door, a second version of Marie appeared in front of her, blocking her exit.

"What are you?" the duplicate asked.

The woman looked between the two Maries, then

turned so she was focused on the original one. Locking her beady eyes on the witch, she waved her knobby hands at Marie while murmuring something in another language. Latin, perhaps. At the end of her chant, she flicked her hands toward the original Marie and a burst of light exploded from them and showered over the witch.

The second version of Marie dissipated and the woman took the opportunity to scurry out of the exhibit.

Marie stood, stunned. She extended her arms and looked herself over, before determining that she was okay. Then she turned toward the boy and rushed to him.

"Are you okay?"

The boy nodded, although he still looked terrified.

"Where are your parents?"

"I…I…I don't know."

She nodded and helped him up. "Come on. Let's see if we can find them."

As she led him to the exhibit exit, a frantic woman rushed over and scooped the boy up in her arms.

"There you are!" She hugged him tight and then took his face in her hands. "Are you okay?"

The boy nodded, tears still wet on his face. "Can we go home?"

"Yes, honey. Of course." The woman turned to

Marie. "Thank you for helping him."

Marie smiled. "No problem. I'm glad he's okay."

As the boy walked off, Marie watched them leave. She couldn't help but wonder what that strange woman was doing in the exhibit with him. And she was going to find out.

CHAPTER 4

Levi Meyer was back in business. With Meyer's Place fixed up from the supernatural attack a few weeks earlier, the restaurant—and the basement speakeasy—were back and crowded with customers.

"Frankie!" he called when the witch and the oracle returned. "Could you take care of Table 4? They just got here."

Taking an apron from the hook just behind the bar, Frankie stepped right into action.

Part of his arrangement with Levi was that he would fill in at the restaurant in exchange for a free room up above the restaurant. Levi also gave him a small paycheck, but nothing substantial. Both of them liked the arrangement for many reasons. For one, Frankie could work the restaurant or the speakeasy and not be traced as an employee, which he had no legitimate papers to verify. And two, when Frankie found a way home, any work he offered Levi would end, leaving Levi on the line to hire a replacement. The money Levi saved in trading a room for work helped him save toward Frankie's eventual replacement.

As Frankie took the order for a couple of businessmen, he couldn't help but think about how different his life had turned out. Prior to getting lost in the 20s, he was a real estate agent and a father. Now, he was a server at the whim of a man who was nearly twenty years younger than him.

But, he could've had things worse. He could've been looking for a job and a place to stay. At least those two things were taken care of. And Levi was a good boss because he was a good friend.

The lunch time rush died off after about an hour. Evelyn sat at the end of the bar, drinking a glass of Coca-Cola and reading the newspaper when Frankie came up and took the seat beside her. Levi stood on the other side, wiping the bar top.

"Thanks for filling in," Levi said. "I know you weren't on the schedule to work today, but we got a bigger rush than I thought."

"You've been doing pretty well since you reopened," Frankie said.

"That's a good thing, but I thought it'd take me longer to get back up to my regular business. The restaurant and downstairs are both packed most days. It's hard to keep up."

"Well, I'm here to help." Frankie looked over at the paper Evelyn was reading. It was the *Erie Daily Times*. The headline read: *Prominent businessman, Charles Bennett, dead by suicide*. "Who's Charles Bennett?" he asked.

"He's a real estate bigshot," Levi said. "Just within the last year, this guy made a ton of money."

Evelyn flattened the paper and looked up at both men. "He wasn't doing too hot with the business, then all of a sudden he was making one good deal after the next. Investment properties, rental houses, building lots, you name it. The guy had his fingers in everything."

"And this all happened in the last year?" Frankie asked. "And then he just went and killed himself?"

Evelyn nodded. "His wife found him this morning, I guess. They hadn't even been married for a year."

"So he got rich, met a woman, and married her all in the last year?"

Levi nodded. "The wedding was a pretty big deal too. Lots of coverage."

"That's…unusual." Frankie was at a loss for words.

LUCKY BY MAGIC

"That was my thought too," Evelyn said. "Of course, there's been rumors that he's been gambling too, but there isn't a race track in Erie and going to Buffalo or Cleveland is too far to go regularly, especially if he's new to his wealth. Any gambling money he made must've been at places like the one Levi's got in his basement right now."

Levi cast a glance over at the two guys chatting at the end of the bar. They smoked their cigars and talked in croaky voices about business. Never once had they asked the code word to be allowed entry into the basement.

"So why would he kill himself if he was doing so well?" Frankie asked.

"That's a good question," Evelyn said. "I've always had a suspicion that his wealth was gained supernaturally."

Frankie leaned in closer and lowered his voice. "You think he's a witch?"

She shrugged. "No idea. I never got close enough to get a good vibe on him. Nor have I really cared enough. But this suicide is strange. Seems like he either dabbled in something he didn't know how to control, or he got involved with someone who took advantage of him."

"Is this something we need to fix?" Levi asked.

Both the oracle and the witch looked at him.

"What?" he asked. "We've done some stuff in the past. Helped a genie-vampire escape a sorcerer."

"One time," Frankie clarified. "That's it."

"It's only been one time for the three of us, but you said yourself that you've faced stuff like this in the past, right?"

Frankie shrugged and nodded. "That's true, but—"

"Look, someone is *dead*," Levi cut in. "If Evelyn's suspicion is correct and someone targeted him, then isn't it within your responsibility to help them? And if I'm willing to help you…?"

Frankie turned to Evelyn for help, but she just shrugged.

"He has a point."

"Great!" Levi said with a smile. "So where do we start?"

"*You* keep working," Frankie said. "I think this starts with Evelyn, simply because of her power."

She nodded. "I'm going to go to my usual table downstairs and see if this headline will help spark any sort of reading on Charles Bennett. If he *did* get supernatural assistance in any way, then we'll need to check to make sure that whatever—or whoever—he used is gone for good and that the dying ends with Charles."

CHAPTER 5

No matter what time period Frankie was in, one thing remained: the errands of everyday life looked more or less the same. Frankie stood in line at the Marine National Bank on State and 9th Streets, waiting to make a deposit for Meyer's Place on Levi's behalf.

The lobby of the bank was very grand and ornate. Back when these institutions wanted to give off the perception of wealth so that people would invest their money in the bank. It also added to the city's architecture, which was one of the finer details Frankie enjoyed about being stuck in 1924.

Toward the windows overlooking the street, Frankie

heard two people talking. Or rather, one man making a scene while the woman tried to maintain her composure. Frankie had noticed them when he had first walked in, but didn't pay them much mind until their conversation escalated. Now, nearly everyone in the lobby was pretending to *not* hear them.

But even though they were being loud, Frankie still couldn't decipher what exactly they were talking about. The man was hysterical and the woman seemed cold. He was begging her to reconsider, but neither of them specified as to what that was.

When the man burst into sobs, Frankie and the woman in line behind him both turned to look in his direction. He sat at a bench near the windows overlooking the street and had his head buried in his hands.

"I don't know what I'm going to do! I have nothing left! I can't go home to my wife with this! She'll leave me for sure!"

The woman with him took the seat beside him. Frankie was surprised by their pairing. She was very put together in her white dress and hat, while the man was very unkempt. Shirt untucked, hair standing on end, tie hanging loose around his neck.

"I know, I know," she said in tones that didn't convey generosity.

She's nicer than I am, Frankie thought to himself. *I would probably just walk out and let him be.*

Frankie exchanged a look with the woman standing behind him and raised his eyebrows to convey their shared annoyance at the disturbance during their mundane errand. After she returned the gesture, he turned and faced forward again, taking one step ahead as he moved forward in line.

"Your luck has run out," the woman in the white dress said to the crying man. "But I believe that has changed. You and I can work out an arrangement."

Really? Frankie thought. *A hooker picking up a guy in the middle of a bank? In 1924? Then again, it is the oldest profession, so I guess they would be in any time period. And why not a bank? She'd probably find a man with a fat wallet quick enough.*

"Can I help you?" the teller called to Frankie. He stepped forward and made the deposit. It wasn't a large amount. Inflation hadn't kicked up to 1984 standards yet, but Levi seemed happy with how much he was making and he knew his finances better than anyone else.

With the errand complete, Frankie turned toward the door as he folded the written receipt and slipped it in his pocket. He looked up just in time to stop short of running into the woman in white at the door. She paused and waved her hand to indicate that he could exit first.

Two things struck Frankie at the same time. The first was how beautiful she was. The second was that she looked familiar, but he couldn't place how, exactly.

He stepped outside and held the door open for her. "After you," he said with a smile.

She winked at him as she stepped through. "Thank you. Such a gentleman."

Her familiarity nagged at him and he considered asking her if they'd ever met before. She walked down State Street and disappeared into the bustling crowd. He didn't get the chance to ask her why she looked familiar, however, when his attention was pulled by someone else exiting the bank. It was the man she had been talking to.

There were no more tears on his face, though. This time, he was elated. He had a wad of cash in his hand, which he counted greedily, oblivious to his surroundings. He stepped right off the curb and into the street.

"Hey!" Frankie hesitated in the crowd before using his power. This wasn't 1984. State Street was packed with people. If he exposed himself as a witch, it would bring loads of unwanted attention. Still, he couldn't let the man die.

An oncoming streetcar rang its bell to warn the man. Brakes squealed as the streetcar tried to stop in time. Finally looking up, the man stopped in his tracks in the gap between the passing streetcar and a car whipping by in the opposite direction. Both moving vehicles narrowly missed the man and, after they each passed, he safely crossed to the other side of the street.

The whole interaction surprised Frankie. That had been a near-miss. That man was lucky that he hadn't been hit. And that sudden wad of cash he had, after spending several minutes crying to some woman about needing her help?

Frankie looked down the sidewalk to where the woman had walked off to, but he couldn't spot her either. He suddenly had a suspicion that there was something supernatural going on. What had happened in that bank?

CHAPTER 6

Samantha and Kathy both squealed as they jumped around the yard, through the water spraying from the hose that they had propped up against an aluminum lawn chair.

Marie lay back in a lounge chair just outside the kitchen. She had *The Art of Magic* propped up on her legs as she casually flipped through the book. She had been trying to find that woman she had encountered at the zoo, but so far she hadn't had any luck.

"There you all are." Frankie stepped through the backdoor in his work clothes.

The girls ran to him to give him a hug and he scooped them up, not minding one bit that they were cold and wet.

"Did you two have fun at the zoo today?" he asked.

"Yeah!" Samantha said. "We saw all kinds of animals."

He smiled. "That's great! You didn't give Mommy a hard time, did you?"

"No, but I think Grandma and Grandpa needed a nap," she said.

Kathy nodded beside her. She still hadn't completely found her voice, so she often agreed to whatever her sister said.

Frankie laughed. "Yeah, well, I bet they probably take naps whether they've spent the day at the zoo or not."

"Are we going to eat dinner soon?" Kathy asked.

"Probably. I still have to talk to your mother about it. Why don't you girls keep playing out here for a few minutes before you dry off and get dressed. Sound like a plan?"

Kathy nodded and stuck her thumb up in the air, then turned and chased her sister back to the hose.

Frankie lifted Marie's legs into his lap as he took a seat at the end of the lounge chair. "Hello, darling." He leaned forward and kissed her. "How was the zoo?"

She sighed. "It was good. I'm glad your parents were there, though. I think we all enjoyed our time better when the adults outnumbered the kids."

"That's good." He looked down at the magic book as he absently rubbed her legs. "What's this for?"

"Research." She had finally found the page with the woman. Her name was Morta, but she hadn't read much further than that. She closed the book so as not to pique her husband's curiosity—or rather, his worry. "I ran into someone at the zoo today and wanted to check up on them."

Frankie dropped his voice lower. "Someone bad?"

Marie shrugged. "That's what I'm guessing. She was giving a little boy a hard time. Targeting him or something. But I was able to stop her and return the boy to his mother, so it all worked out fine."

"Then why were you checking the book?"

"Just curious as to who she was, but it really doesn't matter now. Everyone is safe."

"Did the girls see any of it?"

She shook her head. "No, they were with your parents, eating lunch. Honestly, I didn't even mention it to your parents because it was so insignificant."

Frankie eyed her suspiciously. "Typically when something is insignificant it means that we were able to kill them properly. Sounds like this woman just ran off."

"Empty handed," Marie amended. She took her husband's face in her hands and looked right into his eyes. "Trust me. It's fine. Nothing to worry about."

Lucky by Magic

"If you say so, my dear." He leaned in and kissed her again.

"Did you want to grill up those sausages for dinner?" she asked to change the subject. "We still have some leftover from what your parents gave us. If not, I can make something else."

Frankie stood up and stretched. "No, that's okay. It's still nice out, so we should enjoy the weather. Do you mind starting the grill while I go up and change? And, while I'm out here cooking, I can keep an eye on the girls if you need a break."

She laughed. "Yes, I would very much appreciate a little alone time today."

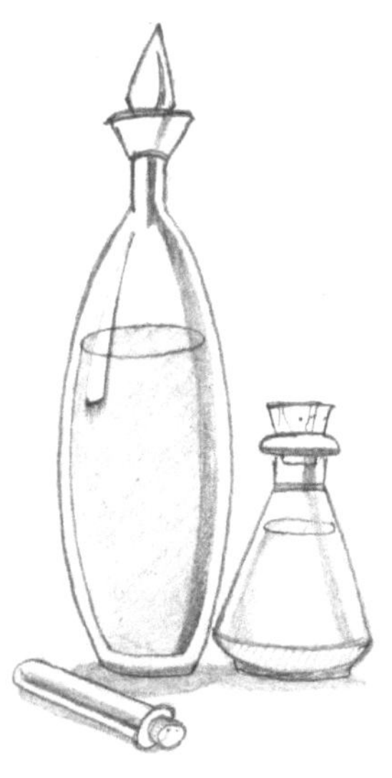

CHAPTER 7

"Okay, so let me get this straight: you saw someone *almost* die and that makes you think there's something magical going on?" Levi asked back at the restaurant. The place was quiet, between mealtime rushes, and Levi busied himself with cleaning up and restocking silverware and condiments.

"It was a very close call." Frankie had just finished telling Levi what he had seen at the bank.

"People get lucky all the time like that."

Frankie shook his head. "You didn't see it. If he had been even an inch closer—in either direction—he would've been hit. It's too big of a coincidence."

Levi still looked skeptical.

Lucky by Magic

"Let's see what Evelyn says, then," Frankie told him. "She'll agree with me."

"She's still downstairs, trying to get a reading on Charles Bennett. There's someone else who had had a string of good luck before he killed himself. You think the two are connected? If what you say is anything to sneeze at, of course. Still doesn't sound like much to me, but I'm not the witch here."

"I guess they could be related. None of it sits quite right with me."

"What doesn't sit right with you?" Evelyn emerged from the back room where the staircase to the speakeasy was hidden.

"Frankie saw a guy walk into traffic and survive and he thinks it's supernatural."

The witch shot him a look. "That's not exactly what happened. He almost got hit by a streetcar and a passing car at exactly the same moment, but somehow managed to miss them both."

"Lucky." She took the seat beside him.

"Too lucky. And before that, he was in the bank crying to some woman—who looked familiar somehow—about how he needed her help with something. I would guess something to do with money, based on the location." He shook his head. "I wish I could remember where I know that woman from."

"From this time period or your own?" Levi asked.

"I'm not sure. I feel like it's this one, though."

"So what happened with this guy?" Evelyn asked.

"I mean, not much, I guess. He was crying to this woman in the bank, then by the time I was done, he had a stack of cash and seemed pretty happy. Total turnaround in his mood. That's when he walked into the street and almost died."

"But he didn't," Evelyn said. "What did he do after that? Was he surprised?"

"Sure he was, but then he just walked off. Like the cash he had won was more important."

"If he was so worried about money that he was crying in public, then yeah, getting some money would distract him from anything else," Levi said.

"But where did the cash come from?" Frankie asked. "It all happened in a matter of minutes."

"I think we need to focus more on this woman he was talking to," Evelyn said. "She may be the key."

"How do you figure?"

"From what I saw in my readings, Charles Bennett's good luck *was* supernatural," she explained. "I'm just not sure how, exactly. But one thing that I *did* see was that he had had contact with a beautiful blonde woman. That could be the same woman that Frankie saw today."

"So we need to figure out what happened," Frankie

said. "Because we can't let anyone else have anymore close calls like I saw today. Especially if luck *isn't* on their side."

Levi looked between the two of them. "What are you going to do? March down to the police station and ask for information on Charles Bennett's suicide? They wouldn't give you the time of day."

Frankie looked down and smirked. Sometimes it really was that easy for him, back in 1984. He could usually pump his friend Gary for information casually over lunch. It would help Frankie solve whatever magical mystery he had on his hands at the time and it wouldn't tip off Gary to his probing.

Those days were over, though.

"Of course we're not going to the police," Evelyn said. "But we could talk to Bennett's widow."

"I don't know," Levi said hesitantly. "Wouldn't that look odd if a couple of strangers start asking about the guy's sudden suicide? I mean, they might even be looking at the wife as a suspect, if they suspect it was murder."

"No, it's actually a great idea," Frankie chimed in. "She'll be able to account for his actions over the last year, when he had good luck. Maybe she can even note any changes to his behavior that showed that his luck had turned."

"This is one of those things you two are going to do no matter what I say, isn't it?" Levi asked.

Evelyn waved it off as she got to her feet. "Don't you worry about us. We'll be fine. Let's go, Frankie."

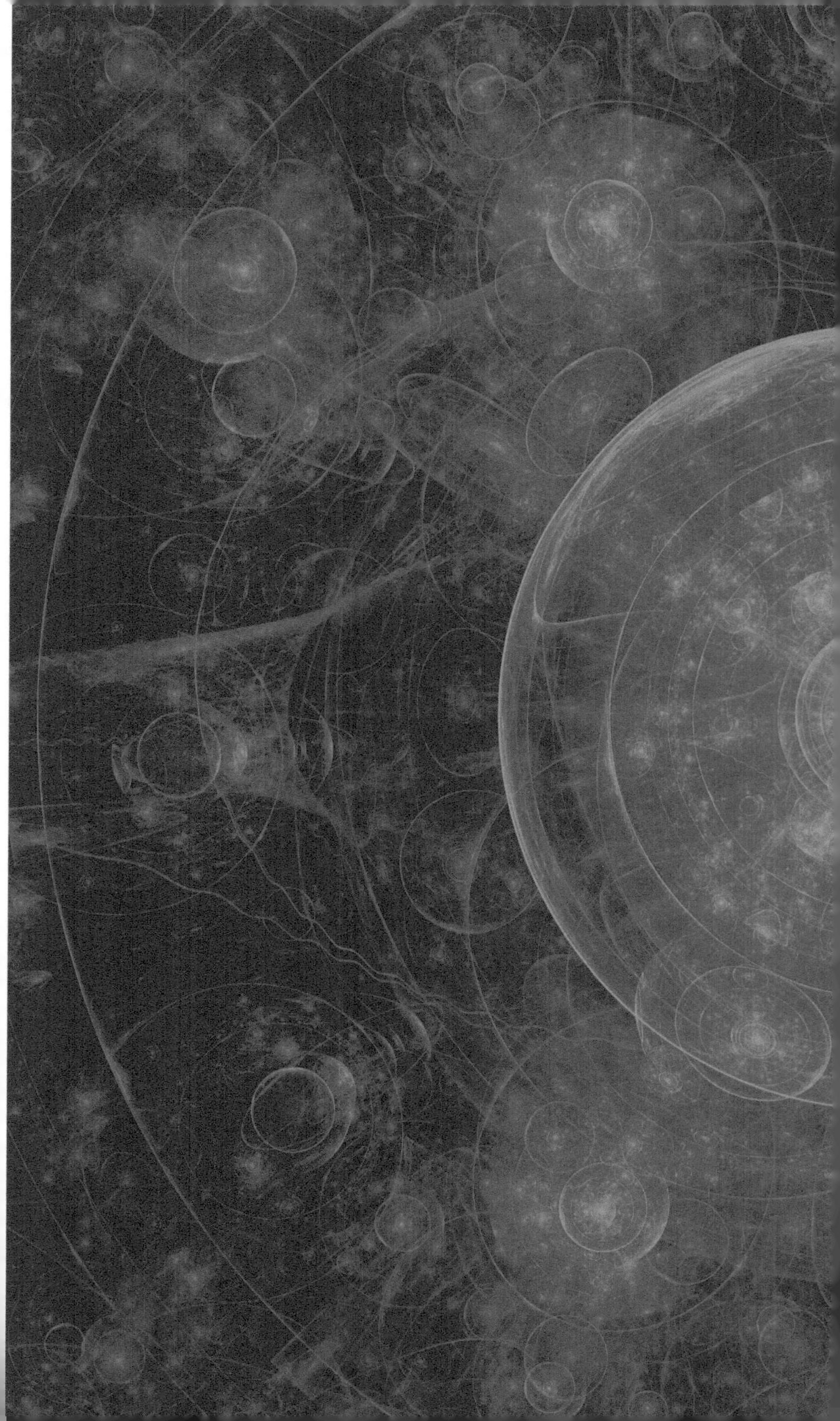

Chapter 8

"What's the plan?" Frankie asked as they walked down West 6th Street.

"We need to ask her about her husband's sudden fortune," Evelyn said.

"Right, but we're not just going to walk up to her and start asking questions. We need to give her a story that would make her want to tell us those things." Frankie already knew that asking her about her husband's fortune would likely be different questions from what the police had already asked her, which would work in their favor.

"Okay, so what story are we going to give her?"

They were standing on the front doorstep of a large

brick home. It was grand, matching many of the other houses in the neighborhood in its elegance. The garden was perfectly landscaped. The steps were swept clean of any debris.

The whole street gave off the impression that people with money lived here, which was probably true. There were large shade trees overhanging both the street and the sidewalk, and a gentle breeze moved through, creating an idyllic atmosphere.

The door suddenly swung open and a woman a few years younger than Frankie stood on the other side. "Can I help you?"

"Uh…" Evelyn stammered.

"We're grief counselors," Frankie blurted. "Are you the widow of Mr. Charles Bennett?" He could feel Evelyn's eyes on him as he met the woman's.

"Yes. My name is Catherine. I've never heard of such a thing as a grief counselor."

Frankie gave her a sad smile and nodded slowly. "Yes, unfortunately we're a rather small industry. We're here to help people, such as yourself, cope with loss. My condolences for your husband."

"Thank you," Catherine said softly. She was clearly still confused.

"May we come in?" Evelyn asked. "To speak with you privately? We want to help."

"Okay. Yes, come in." Catherine stepped aside to allow them entry.

The house was as beautiful inside as it was outside. Surprisingly, it seemed even larger on the inside. The hardwood floors were covered in strategic areas by oriental rugs that defined the spaces, along with the larger furnishings. The furniture was all hand-crafted and elegant. The walls were lined with oak panels. Even the light fixtures had amazing details to them.

"Why don't we take a seat in the den?" Catherine led them to a front room overlooking the street. "Would you like some tea?"

Frankie and Evelyn both sat on the velvet-lined couch near the window.

"Yes, that would be nice," he said.

"I'll be just a moment." Catherine disappeared. In the next room, they could hear her faintly calling for the help. "Petunia! Petunia, where are you? We have guests!"

In her absence, Evelyn leaned toward Frankie. "Grief counselors?"

"It's a thing where I'm from."

"I gathered that."

Catherine came back in and took a seat in the chair across from them. "Petunia will be right in with our tea."

"Thank you," Evelyn said.

LUCKY BY MAGIC

"Mrs. Bennett," Frankie started.

"You can call me Catherine." She offered a sad smile. "After all, we're about to talk about my husband's suicide."

"Catherine." He smiled at her, an attempt to further disarm her if she raised any objections to their questions. "Was there any indication that you saw that your husband was unhappy?"

"None. We were elated. Still in our first year of marriage, although we had been together for years before that." She looked down and played with her wedding ring. "He always said that I deserved the world and he wouldn't propose to me until he had enough money to buy me a ring and a wedding that I truly loved. And when that time finally came, he wasted no expense."

"I didn't realize you two were together before you got married," Evelyn said.

Catherine nodded. "For years, actually. He was the boy in my neighborhood who caught my eye and we've been nearly inseparable ever since."

"Were you happy?" Frankie asked, playing up the grief counselor role. Although, he had no idea what he was doing in that department. Luckily, Catherine didn't know that. "Before he came into some money?"

"Absolutely," she said without hesitation. "He had my heart long before money even became a consideration for us. Obviously, as we got older, we struggled. Charles never could seem to make the right deal. Every time he thought he had a sure thing, something would come along to mess it up. And he was always so sure that he would put more money than we had into these deals. For a while, we were in some hot water. Worse than I probably even knew."

"What do you mean by hot water?" Evelyn asked.

"Charles…owed some people some money. Bad people, from what I understand. He never talked about it much. At least, not to me. However, he seemed agitated. Stressed. As more and more business deals didn't turn out, he became more defeated in a way that had me worried." Her eyebrows raised as she stared at the floor. "*Very* worried."

"Do you think these people are the reason he decided to…?" Evelyn let her question hang.

"Oh, no. Certainly not. I confronted Charles about owing money to people. He wouldn't tell me everything, but he said enough that I knew I was right in my assumptions. He promised me he'd turn it around. And he did! Suddenly, he was making fantastic investments and earning his money back. He paid those men back—with interest—and was still able to walk away from them with more than enough money for us." She looked at her ring again. "The first thing he did after his debtors were paid off was propose to me with this ring."

They were interrupted by a young black woman who wore a traditional maid outfit and carried a silver tray with a teapot, cups, and small dishes for sugar, milk, and honey.

"Oh, thank you, Petunia," Catherine said to her as she set it on the table in the center of the room.

"Is there anything else you need, miss?"

Catherine reached for her hand and squeezed it. "No, that is enough for now. Thank you." Sitting on the edge of her seat, Catherine poured cups for her guests. "Please, help yourself to fix it any way you like."

"Catherine, part of our job is to help you make sense of what happened," Frankie started after he had poured his tea. "But what I'm confused about is that after your husband came into some money and paid off his debtors, he didn't seem to have any reason for any turmoil. Was he haunted by some other demons that weren't related to money?"

"No..." The widow took a sip and looked down. "Well...he did have a, um...*nervous* energy to him. Especially closer to...the end."

"Nervous how?" Evelyn asked.

"He wanted to make sure that he had surefire investments lined up so that we'd always be taken care of." She frowned. "Although, the idea of 'we' always seemed to come second. He would say things like, 'I want to make sure *you're* taken care of' or 'This money needs to last your whole life.' He seemed to know that he wouldn't be around forever."

"How would he know that?" Evelyn asked.

Frankie marked the irony in that statement, of an oracle questioning someone else's potential clairvoyance.

"Maybe it wasn't that he *knew*," Catherine clarified. "But he seemed sure that his good luck in business wouldn't last. When I asked him about it, he always said that nothing is a guarantee. That we had to plan for failure so it doesn't kick us in the end."

"That's true," Frankie said.

"But he was so smart with his money once he had it," Catherine persisted. "Stocks, secure business deals, savings accounts, even stashes of cash throughout the house. It never seemed to be enough, though."

"Catherine, did your husband ever mention…a woman?" Evelyn asked.

The question caused a noticeable shift in the room. Catherine stared at Evelyn with such intensity that Frankie could almost feel the rage radiating off of her.

"Excuse me?"

"Specifically a blonde woman," the oracle went on. "Perhaps she sometimes wore a veil? Dressed in white?"

Frankie watched the interaction quietly. He didn't

want to say anything wrong that would make Catherine feel as though they were ganging up on her with assumptions and insinuations.

"Charles was not unfaithful," Catherine said sternly.

"Of course," Evelyn said. "That's not what I was—"

"He was a good man. A loving husband. He clearly had something he was wrestling with, but to suggest an affair—"

"Mrs. Bennett—" Frankie tried to soothe the widow himself, but she wasn't having it.

"I'd like you both to leave." She rose to her feet and stepped to the doorway.

"Mrs. Bennett, we didn't mean to offend you," Evelyn said. "I was just asking because—"

Frankie put his hand on her shoulder to quiet her. They had heard enough. No sense in tormenting the poor woman any longer.

"We'll let you get back to getting your affairs in order." Frankie stood at the door and waited for Evelyn to catch up.

The oracle trailed her hand along the back of the couch they had been sitting in on her way to the door. She reached for tables and doorframes. No doubt trying to get a vision.

"Thank you for your time," Frankie said to Catherine. "I hope that we have helped in some way."

As the two of them finally made their way out of the house, Catherine closed the door without another word.

Down on the sidewalk, Evelyn reached for Frankie's shirtsleeve to stop him.

"What is it?" Frankie asked.

"I had a vision in there."

"I figured that's what you were trying to do. What did you see?"

"The woman you saw today at the bank? She's at Meyer's Place and she's about to make another deal with someone else."

CHAPTER 9

The usual tricks were not working. Marie sat in Kathy's room and tried to rock her to sleep, but the three-year-old would not give in to her nap. Marie had tried reading her a story, singing to her, and simply just patting her on the back. None of it worked.

She missed the days when Kathy was still in a crib and Marie would just give her a few minutes to cry it out before she fell asleep on her own. With the toddler bed, Kathy would be playing with her toys only moments after Marie left the room, and then be miserable and tired hours before bedtime.

Samantha, meanwhile, had been asleep in her own room for fifteen minutes. It had been a long morning and

Lucky by Magic

Marie very much needed a break from motherhood, even if for only a little while.

Marie held Kathy close as she rocked faster in the chair. Finally, after several more minutes, the squirming toddler began to settle and give in to her exhaustion.

You're a terrible mother.

The thought came to Marie seemingly out of nowhere. Never before had she thought that about herself. And yet, here she was thinking it. Maybe it was even true. After all, she couldn't even get her own daughter to sleep. She was hoping both girls would sleep a long time so she could have time away from them. And she had even contemplated leaving Kathy alone in her room to cry herself to sleep, simply so Marie could have a moment without children.

What kind of mother did that?

The thoughts were brushed aside as Marie realized the house had gone quiet. Kathy had finally fallen asleep.

Easing herself out of the rocker, Marie slowly set Kathy down in her bed and gently pulled the covers over her.

As she came down the stairs, she saw the toys scattered all over the living room. For a second, she considered leaving them and just laying on the couch. But then the thought popped into her head again — *You're a terrible mother* — and she decided to prove herself wrong.

But as she tidied up the house, even more unwanted thoughts made their way into her consciousness.

This place is a mess because you don't pick up enough.

You let these kids run wild.

You should be doing more with them.

Frustrated and feeling a little defeated, Marie finished picking up in the living room and then went into the kitchen, where the few dishes from lunch sat in the sink. Usually, she would wait to wash them with the dinner dishes so she only had to do the dishes once a day, but now she was determined to keep a tidy home *and* take care of the kids.

She put on the radio to tune out any other unwanted thoughts and set to work cleaning up.

Mercifully, she was able to finish cleaning up without beating herself up anymore.

When she was done, Marie went into the living room and collapsed on the couch with the book she had been trying to read for weeks. Usually, she only got to read a full, uninterrupted chapter right before she went to bed. Sometimes, if she was lucky, she could squeeze in one during nap time, but the girls didn't always take naps at the same time, which made it hard.

As she got comfortable on the couch and tried to dive into her book, she heard tiny footsteps on the stairs.

"Mommy?" Samantha called.

LUCKY BY MAGIC

Marie closed her eyes and let out a deep breath. She had *just* sat down.

You're a terrible mother.

She sat up and put on a smile as Samantha walked into the living room, rubbing her eyes. "Did you have a good nap, dear?"

Samantha nodded. "Where's Kathy?"

"Still sleeping."

"Oh. Could we make something in the kitchen?"

Marie had just cleaned the kitchen. But at the risk of the negative thoughts returning, she simply said, "Sure, honey. What do you want to make?"

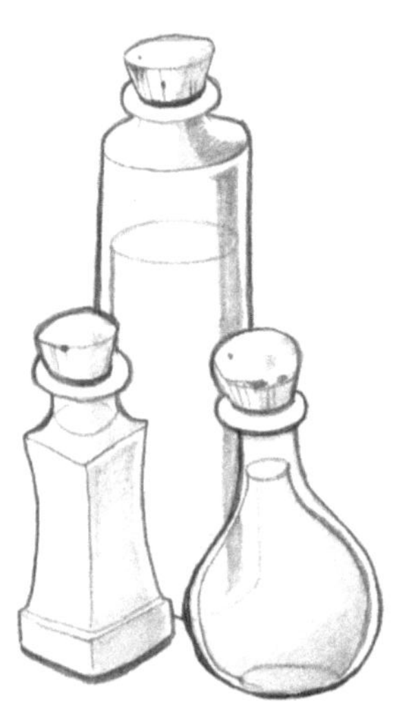

CHAPTER 10

It wasn't a surprise that the woman in white from Evelyn's vision was down in the speakeasy. No matter the time of day, there were usually people down in the basement of Meyer's Place. And when everyone was already keeping the secret of the bar in the midst of prohibition, they tended to keep out of everyone else's other affairs as well.

Frankie and Evelyn took a seat behind the woman. She was seated with a different man, who seemed equally as distraught as the man Frankie had seen at the bank. More than that, the look in his eyes showed not only desperation, but hunger and tiredness as well. Frankie felt bad for him.

LUCKY BY MAGIC

"I need a job," the man said. "We have nothing left in savings. We're already renting out two rooms in our house. My wife has been doing the laundry for people in the neighborhood just to bring in some extra cash to feed our family. I have four kids! Do you know how heart wrenching it is to hear your daughter crying at night because she can't go to sleep for how hungry she is?"

The woman nodded. "That has to be hard."

Although she was saying the right thing, Frankie sensed a lack of true empathy on her part. Her voice sounded flat, disinterested.

The man, however, didn't seem to pick up on it. "I need to be able to provide for them. I'm the man of the house and I have nothing to give. Not since I lost my job."

"Yes, well, unfortunately in my line of work I come across a lot of men who have the same problems as you do. Our country is seeing financial prosperity, but that doesn't mean it's evenly distributed."

"That's exactly what I've been saying!" The man's eyes lit up. "It's like, everyone else seems to be doing well, but I just can't catch a break."

Even from behind, Frankie could tell from the woman's posture that she felt smug with herself.

"I can help you with that."

"You can?"

Another nod. "I can offer you luck. Good luck. Genuine, absolute luck on your side for a full year. Interested?"

"How?"

"I have my ways. What I'm offering you is an opportunity to turn things around. To finally provide for your family."

"And this is only for a year?"

"Trust me, that is all you'll need. After the year is up, the luck will change and I'll come back around to collect." She leaned in close and held up a finger. "However, if you use your luck wisely, you will be able to take care of your family for the rest of their lives."

Evelyn turned to Frankie, horrified at what she had heard. She mouthed, "The rest of *their* lives?"

Frankie knew from Charles Bennett that whenever this woman came to collect, it wouldn't end well. Still, he wanted to hear exactly how the deal was made, so he waved off Evelyn and turned his attention back to the next table.

"You're taking an awfully long time to consider a life-changing opportunity." The woman glanced at her nails as she waited for his response.

The man chewed on his bottom lip as he looked toward the floor. "What do you get out of it?"

"I'll let you know when I come to collect," she said.

Lucky by Magic

He still seemed unsure.

"This is a choice," she said. "It's entirely up to you. Do you want to turn your luck around for your family or do you want to hear your daughter cry at night?"

Low blow, Frankie thought to himself. *She's kicking the man when he's already down. I would do anything for my girls and I'm guessing this man would too.*

"So," the woman asked, "do we have a deal?"

CHAPTER 11

The man paused for only a moment to decide, then he extended his hand toward the woman. "Deal."

The woman shook his hand. "Good choice. And good luck. I wish you well. You should notice the luck taking effect immediately. The clock is ticking."

"Thank you! Thank you!" The man rose to his feet and nearly tripped over his chair—nearly, but didn't actually trip. He managed to get his footing and the chair righted. With an exuberant wave, he ran up the stairs and into his new reality.

The woman remained in her seat and took a slow sip from her drink. As she set it back on the table, she said, "You two can come and talk to me face-to-face. You don't have to pretend like you're not here to spy on me."

Frankie and Evelyn exchanged looks for a brief moment, then both rose and joined the woman at the table.

"Do you want to tell us who you are or is the veil you're hiding behind a symbol for the big ball of mystery you like to operate in?" Frankie asked.

The woman smiled. Her bright white teeth in contrast to her red lipstick. "I've been called lots of things over the years. Fortuna, for instance. Tyche is another. My personal favorite, though, has to be Lady Luck. It sounds so formal and is a name that demands respect. People throw luck around so frivolously. It needs to be recognized and respected."

"You demand respect even when you're killing people?" Evelyn asked.

"Ah ah ah." Lady Luck put up her finger and waved it slightly. "I've never once killed anyone. I merely fulfill my end of the bargain that the two parties both agree to."

"By turning their luck around," Frankie clarified.

"Indeed. Those are the terms we agree to when the deal is made, as you've just witnessed."

"But you never warned him that he could die," Evelyn said.

"Some things are better left unsaid." Lady Luck

smirked. "I wouldn't want to assume the man's ignorance. I'm sure he figured it out on his own. Besides, I've had previous clients whose luck have run out and they're still alive."

"Not many, though." Frankie wasn't surprised by the callousness of this woman. He had seen it many times before. Someone who was so greedy and selfish didn't often think of other people.

She shrugged. "Bad luck. It's the price they pay for having a year of only good luck."

"But that's not fair," Evelyn blurted.

"Neither is having a year full of only good luck."

"That deal you just made with that man never specified how he would have to pay," the oracle pushed.

"Again, I don't want to assume the man's ignorance—"

"Please," Evelyn nearly spat. "You knew exactly how vague you were being."

"If he would've asked, I would've told him," Lady Luck said. "He didn't, so I wasn't obligated to fill him in."

"What about a *moral* obligation?" Evelyn asked.

"Are you trying to kill them?" Frankie added. "Do you *want* your clients to die? Do you collect their souls or something? Is that how this works?"

"I don't collect any souls. I simply distribute luck."

Lucky by Magic

"And you just get off on distributing bad luck to people after teasing them with good luck for a year?" Frankie was pissed.

Lady Luck was getting the same way too. "Look. All I'm doing is giving people what they want. They don't ask for specifics, so I don't offer them. The choice is theirs." She downed the rest of her glass and set it on the table. "Now, if you'll excuse me, I have business to attend to." She rose and started toward the staircase leading upstairs.

Frankie wanted to say something that would stop her from going off and making another bad deal with some defenseless person who was already down on their luck, but he couldn't think of anything. This woman saw nothing wrong with what she was doing, so there was no way to make her stop on her own. And if people were dying, then they needed to find another way to stop her.

With Lady Luck gone, Frankie turned to look at Evelyn, but hesitated when he looked over at her. Instead of shooting daggers at Lady Luck with her eyes like Frankie had been, she was sitting with her eyes closed and her head down. It wasn't until after Lady Luck had disappeared upstairs that she lifted her head.

"What is it?" he asked. "What did you see?"

When the oracle looked at him, there was nothing but worry in her eyes. "Someone else is about to die."

CHAPTER 12

Marie came back into the bedroom after checking on the girls and went to her bottle of lotion on her dresser. She squeezed some on her hand and began rubbing it into her leg.

Frankie sat up in bed with his shirt off, reading the newspaper. She watched him, seeing a man who had it all together. A good family. A house. A good job. Strong powers.

She glanced at the full-length mirror in the corner and saw herself. What did she have to show for her life? What did she truly bring to the marriage? To their family?

Having finished with the lotion, Marie pulled back

the blankets on her side of the bed and sighed as she sat down.

Frankie kept his eyes on the paper, but reached out with one hand to pat her leg. "What's the matter?"

"It's nothing," she said with another sigh as she got comfortable.

He set the paper down and looked at her. "No, tell me."

She pursed her lips and looked down at her nails. "Do you think I do enough?"

"What do you mean?"

"For the girls. For you. For the house."

"Honey, of course you do." He reached for her hand, but she pulled away. "I know all of the hard work you put in around here. It doesn't go unnoticed. If I haven't told you how much I appreciate it, then—"

"No, it's not that. Not you. I know you notice it all, it's just…" She shrugged, letting the thought die off.

"Then what is it?" He folded up the newspaper and tossed it on the floor beside the bed, giving his wife his full attention.

"I don't know. I just feel like I'm not pulling my weight." She waved it off. "It's stupid. Never mind. Forget I said anything."

This time, he took her hand and held it even when she tried to pull away. After a second, she let him hold it and looked at him.

"Honey, the only reason this house is kept in tip-top shape is because of you," he said. "And not just the housework, the way this family runs is because of you. The girls get where they need to go on time. They're happy. I'm happy. You're the glue that keeps us all together. It might seem like unglamorous work, but don't doubt for a second how important your role is. You keep this house running. Without you, we'd all fall apart."

Marie offered him a sad smile. "You're right. Thanks for the pep talk."

Frankie still wasn't satisfied. "Where did that idea even come from?"

"I don't know. It's just been a hard day with the girls, I guess. I'm just in a mood." She shrugged. "Been feeling like I'm not enough."

He scooted closer to her in bed and wrapped his arms around her. She leaned in and rested her head on his shoulder.

"Never for a second think that you're not enough," he told her. "You're everything to me and to our daughters. I don't know what I would do without you. You're perfect for us."

She squeezed him back. "Thank you."

They held each other for a while, neither of them

saying anything, both of their minds racing with different thoughts.

Finally, Marie pulled away. "Come on. We should get some sleep. We all have to be up early tomorrow. The girls have their doctor appointments."

They kissed and said goodnight.

With the lights out, Marie lay in bed and tried to surrender to sleep. But her mind was bombarded with even worse thoughts than she'd been having all day.

You're no good.

Frankie's lying to you.

He's only being nice.

The girls don't like you. They only see you as someone who yells.

Frankie wishes you would pull your weight with the finances.

He's embarrassed you don't have a job.

He's embarrassed of you.

CHAPTER 13

"Whoa! Whoa! Whoa! Where are you guys heading off to?" Levi asked from behind the bar in the dining room.

Frankie and Evelyn slowed their quick pursuit out at the sound of his voice. The place was empty, which explained why Levi was sitting at a high-top chair with the newspaper spread out on the counter in front of him.

"Lady Luck is about to strike again," Frankie said.

"Lady who?"

"We don't have time!" Evelyn said. "We need to go *now*!"

Levi jumped from his chair and came around the counter. "Then I'm going with you."

Lucky by Magic

Frankie looked to Evelyn to make sure it was safe for someone without powers to go. He hadn't seen the vision—or heard much else about it—so he didn't know what they were walking into.

"Hurry up," she told Levi.

They raced out the door. Levi barely had time to flip the sign over to "Closed" before they were gone.

On the sidewalk, Frankie asked, "So where exactly are we going?"

"I'm not sure," she admitted. "I saw a man stuck on the railroad tracks with an oncoming train. I couldn't make out exactly where, but I figured these tracks here would be a good enough place to start."

She led them down Turnpike Street and under the railroad tracks. Right before they reached Peach Street, she started climbing up the embankment to the top of the steel railroad bridges crossing over the street.

"Help!" they heard a man calling. "Help me! I'm stuck!"

"This way!" Evelyn called out frantically as she tried to hurry up the slope.

Frankie and Levi raced up behind her.

At the top, they saw the man in the center of the railroad tracks. His foot was lodged between the railroad tie and the steel track. In the distance, they could see an oncoming train approaching. It was moving slower than normal, being that it was passing through the city, but it was still going fast enough to kill the man if they couldn't get him out of there in time.

"Use your power!" Evelyn told Frankie.

The witch shook his head. "That would derail the whole train. Potentially kill more people and cause all kinds of damage. We need to get him out of there ourselves."

Evelyn rushed to the man's aid, careful to step around the tracks so she didn't get stuck herself.

Behind them, the train blared its horn in warning.

"Why is it always trains?" Levi asked.

"You're okay." Frankie told the man. "We'll get you out of here. Just hold on."

"What about using your power on him?" Levi suggested.

"Can't. I'd break his ankle."

"Power?" the man asked. "What power?"

Evelyn ignored the man's question. "At least he'd be alive." She cast a worried look over her shoulder. "We don't have much time!"

Levi stepped up and grabbed the man's leg. "Help me pull!" He told him. They counted down from three, putting all of their strength into pulling him free.

His leg still didn't budge.

"It's not working!" the man cried.

Lucky by Magic

Frankie surveyed the distance between them and the train. They only had seconds left. "I have an idea."

"Do it quick," Evelyn said.

Standing to the side, Frankie focused on the steel track where the man's foot was stuck and moved his fingers toward himself. Nothing happened at first. He tried again and the steel track moved only a fraction, which allowed enough space for the man to free his leg.

"Got it!" Levi shouted.

Evelyn grabbed both his arm and the man's arm and pulled them down on top of her on the stone beside the tracks. All four of them crumpled down as the train passed by with a roar of its engine.

Frankie watched anxiously as the train whipped by. Once it was out of the way, he let out the breath he'd been holding and relaxed. "That was close."

Evelyn sized them all up. "Too close."

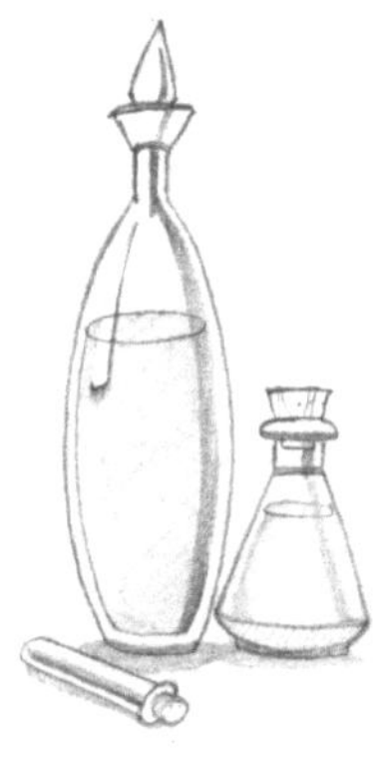

CHAPTER 14

- WEDNESDAY, SEPTEMBER 17, 1924 -

"Sorry about this," Patrick, the man they just saved, said at the bar at Meyer's Place. "I'm still kind of shaken up about the whole thing. If you guys hadn't…"

"But we did," Frankie said.

"And it's a good thing for it, too," Patrick said.

"Can I get you anything to drink?" Levi offered. "Water? Tea? Coffee?"

"Bourbon?" Patrick asked with a laugh. "Nah, I'm fine."

"Patrick," Evelyn started. "We need to ask you some questions. About…a woman."

He looked at her with his eyebrows scrunched together. "A woman?"

Lucky by Magic

"She's blonde, wears all white—and a hat with a veil," she started.

"She likely was someone who promised to change your luck around this time last year," Frankie added. "Goes by Lady Luck, Fortuna, or Tyche."

"Did you see her today?" Evelyn pushed.

Patrick stared at the counter and shook his head. "No, not today. I haven't seen her since last year. Didn't talk much about luck, from what I can remember. Although, my memory is terrible." He paused for a second, then added, "Wait a minute. I did see her. A couple days ago. She showed up at this…*establishment* I was at." He looked up at them, determining whether they understood his subtle substitution of words. "Mentioned something about our deal expiring or something. I don't know. Can't remember too well. I was, um, not quite *myself*, if you catch my drift. Anyway, I don't ever remember making a deal so I just brushed it off. And then I got stuck on the tracks—I never get stuck on the tracks."

"What were you doing up there anyway?" Levi leaned against the back counter.

"I always use the train tracks to cut across town. It's faster than stopping at all those intersections with the lights and the crowd and the cars."

"And you didn't think about how dangerous that could be?" Levi asked.

Patrick shrugged. "I've never gotten hurt."

"No close calls?" Frankie asked. He sat beside Patrick.

"I mean, there were a few, but I always managed to free myself. Even today wasn't terrible, when it really comes down to it. This was the closest call, though. You think maybe that lady was telling the truth about some deal? No money was exchanged or anything. I didn't sign any contracts. Not that I know of anyway. You think she forged my signature?"

"The jury's still out on that her," Evelyn said.

"Why don't you sit tight," Frankie suggested. "The three of us need to discuss some things."

Patrick began to get up. "Nah, I'm okay. Thanks for helping me. I really do owe you one. Listen, if you ever find yourselves in need of a tune-up, I'm working as a mechanic at my brother's garage. It's small, run out of his alleyway garage, but we do good work."

Frankie shook his head. "No thanks. None of us have cars."

"Ah, well. Thought I could drum up some business." He started to the door. "You folks take care. And thanks again. I guess you three saved my life."

"You guess?" Levi murmured, but Frankie shot him a look.

"Be careful!" Evelyn called after Patrick as he walked out.

UCKY BY MAGIC

"You don't see misfortune in his future, do you?" Levi asked Evelyn after they were alone.

"Not that I could tell, but with his luck all messed up I don't know if I'd be able to see it coming in time," she said. "We were almost too late on the train tracks."

"I think I remember why Lady Luck looks so familiar," Frankie said. "I saw her coming out of my grandparents' house this morning."

Evelyn leaned on her fist on the counter and nodded. "Mm-hmm. I thought about that."

"And you didn't think it'd be a good idea to remind me of that? If she went and talked to one of my grandparents, that could put *me* in danger, if it disrupts the timeline."

"I didn't want to say anything because I didn't want you to go back there and potentially *mess up* the timeline."

"Okay, but if Lady Luck was there this morning, that means that she probably struck a deal with one of my grandparents—and I'm guessing it's probably my grandmother, seeing how it was in the middle of the morning and my grandfather would've been working. Not to mention the fact that my *father* will be born two months from now, meaning that she's very pregnant and therefore very vulnerable."

"Even if she made a deal with Lady Luck, that

doesn't mean your grandmother is in immediate danger," Evelyn reasoned. "It means we have a year of her having *good luck*. That means we have time for your father to be born and then Lady Luck will come after *her* and not *him*, which means that you're still safe. If anything, she's safer now that she was before she even struck that deal."

"That's not good enough! We need to warn Anna now!"

Levi stuck his fingers in his mouth and whistled loudly. "All right, you two, break it up! Will one of you explain to me what the hell you're talking about?"

Both Frankie and Evelyn started talking at once.

"He almost exposed his secret to his grandparents—"

"My grandparents live in the house I still live in back in my time—"

"—which would rupture a hole in the timeline—"

"—my grandmother is pregnant with my grandfather and she had a visit from Lady Luck today—"

"—and ruin things for the way things are and will be—"

"—who is making deals with people to give them good luck for a year and then gives them very bad luck, which leads to their death—"

Lucky by Magic

"—his thinking was just so shortsighted and stupid that proved that he *wasn't* thinking—"

"Okay!" Levi bellowed, then stuck his fingers in his mouth and whistled again. Both Frankie and Evelyn went silent. "Sheesh, you're both acting like little kids right now."

"We're not—" Frankie started, but Levi put up his hand to stop him.

"I'm calling a timeout," he said. "Now, hear me out. If this Lady Luck person is giving people good luck and then yanking it all away after a year without necessarily *informing* them that's what she's doing, then I think it's a good idea to warn Anna about the deal that she made with her."

"But—" Evelyn started, but Levi shushed her in the same way he did Frankie.

"I also think it's important that we help the people who will be Lady Luck's next targets. The ones whose deals are about to expire. Evelyn, with your power you're the most suited to figure out who those people are and make sure they're safe. Frankie and I will go and warn Anna."

"But introducing Frankie to Anna could cause serious effects on the timeline," Evelyn warned.

"That's why I'll go with him to make sure he doesn't say anything stupid."

She crossed her arms and hooked an eyebrow. "Sure you will."

"You'll have to trust us," Levi said. "If this really does cause ripples into the timeline, none of us are going to be more impacted than Frankie."

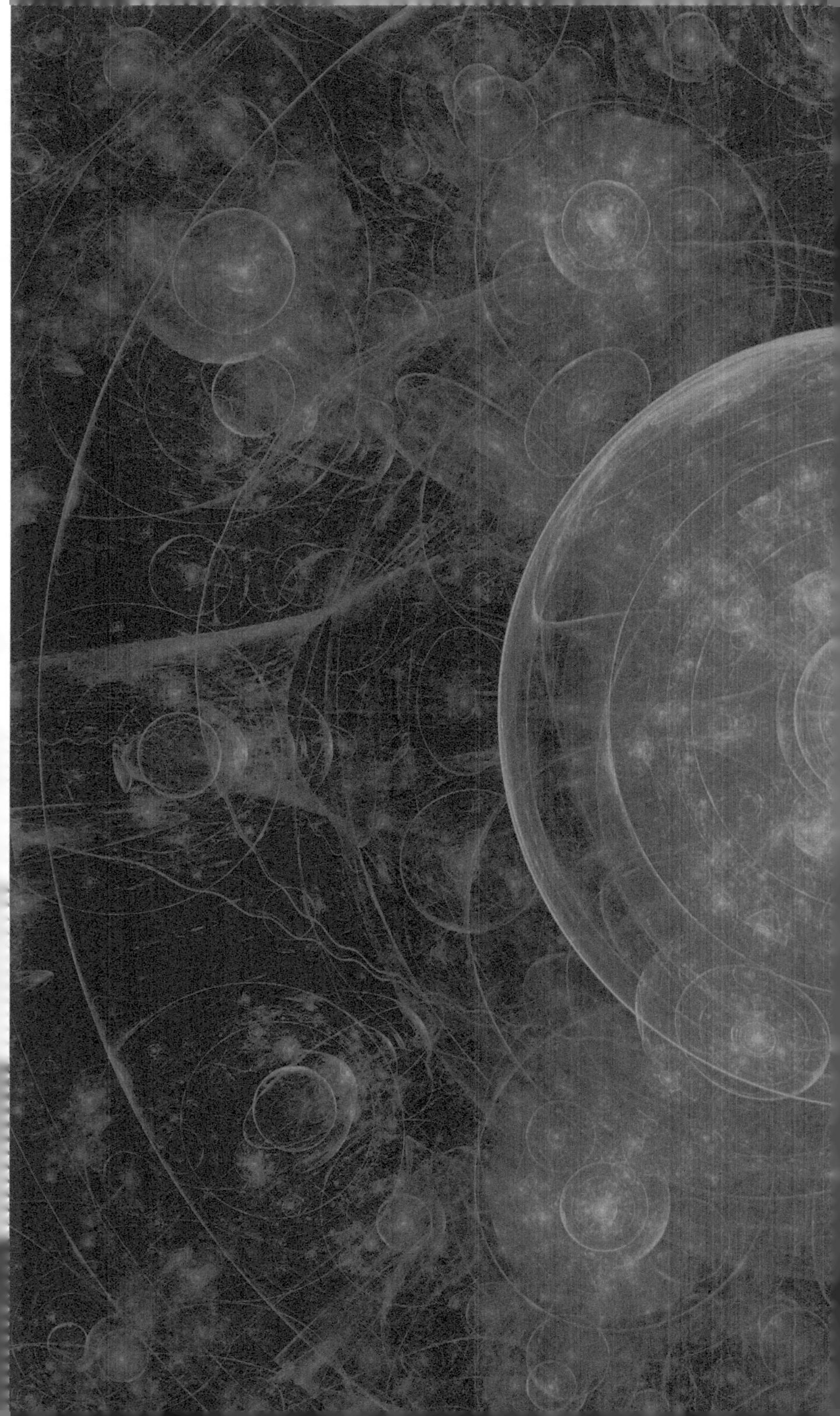

CHAPTER 15

Samantha burst through the front door. "No! I don't want it!"

Marie followed, holding Kathy's hand in hers. "Samantha, you don't have a choice. The medicine will help you."

Samantha was quiet, having found a hiding place somewhere in the house.

Marie let go of Kathy's hand once the front door was closed and went in search of her older daughter. "Samantha, this isn't funny. You have an ear infection. The only way that it's going to get better is if you take your medicine."

"I don't want it!" The angry voice came from the sunroom.

Lucky by Magic

Marie followed the sound and saw Samantha hiding between one of the wicker chairs and the wall of windows. Her back was to Marie and her shoulders shook with sobs. Her right hand absently played with her ear.

"It won't hurt anymore after you take your medicine," Marie said.

Samantha turned and saw her mother, then darted into the living room. "No!"

"Samantha! You get back here right now!" Marie barked. She didn't like yelling at her kids very often, but it had been a rough couple of days and Samantha had been a nightmare at the doctor's office. Whining and squirming in the waiting room, then screaming and crying with the doctor. She even managed to get a good kick into the old man's gut when he tried to administer the first dosage of meds. That's when he suggested that Marie try it at home where Samantha would feel more comfortable.

If only that were true.

"Samantha Walker, I'm *not* kidding around!" Marie hollered again.

At the tone of her mother's voice, Kathy started crying from where she still sat in the foyer.

Marie sighed and went over to her younger daughter and scooped her up in her arms. "I'm sorry, sweetie. Did Mommy scare you?"

Kathy nodded, only a few tears on her face.

"How can I make it up to you?"

She shrugged.

"What if I tickle your belly?" Marie lifted Kathy to her mouth and started blowing on her stomach, to the delightful squeals of her daughter.

With Kathy satisfied, Marie set her back on her feet. "Why don't you pull out some of your toys and play for a while? I need to find your sister and get her to take her medicine."

Kathy nodded and then scampered off to the wooden toy box in the corner of the living room.

Marie grabbed the prescription from her purse that she had picked up from the pharmacy on the way home and went upstairs, where she knew Samantha would be hiding in her room. Very likely under her bed.

"Sam, honey," Marie called. "Please come out. I just want to talk to you."

The door to Samantha's bedroom opened with a squeal of its hinges and the little girl poked her head through the crack.

Marie sat on the floor. "Come here." She set the bottle behind her, out of sight of Samantha. "I just want to explain something to you." If she could reason with her, then maybe Samantha would willingly take the medicine. At least the first dose. She'd have to find a different approach for the second, but by then Frankie would be home and he could help fight the battle alongside her.

Samantha slowly came out of her room and approached her mother in the upstairs landing.

"I just want to talk to you about why it's important to take your medicine."

Samantha stopped and took a half step backward.

"It'll help you feel better," Marie pushed. "You remember how you said it hurt when you laid down in bed? This will make it so your ear doesn't hurt anymore."

Again, the little girl looked cautiously at Marie.

"Come on." Marie waved her over. "Come sit in my lap and you can ask me all of your questions and *then* you can decide if you should take it."

Samantha thought about it and then stepped closer to her mother. When she stepped to the side to sit on Marie's lap, however, she noticed the medicine bottle behind Marie's back and screamed.

Marie grabbed at Samantha, but the little girl was able to wiggle out of her grasp and ran to her room, slamming her door behind her.

Frustrated, Marie scooped up the bottle and chased after Samantha.

"Noooo!" Samantha screamed from under her bed. She kicked her feet wildly, hitting the bottom of the bed frame with each kick.

"Samantha, that's enough! Take the damn medicine or…or your ear's going to fall off!"

Her daughter screamed louder, now afraid of something completely imaginary.

Great parenting, Marie, she thought to herself. But her annoyance outweighed reason. Samantha may have been stubborn, but Marie was going to be more stubborn.

Grabbing ahold of the girl's legs, Marie pulled Samantha out from under the bed and turned her over. She straddled her and when Samantha began smacking at her, Marie pinned her arms down with her knees.

Sitting atop her daughter, Marie held the dropper near Samantha's ear, trying to steady it so she could count the drops. Samantha wiggled her hand out from under her mother and clamped it over her ear, letting out a loud shriek. With each sway of her body, Marie's control over the girl weakened.

Finally, Samantha freed her other hand from under Marie's knee and swatted the medicine away.

Marie watched as it collided with the wall and splattered all over.

Samantha wiggled out from under her mother and

LUCKY BY MAGIC

ran down the stairs, wailing in hysteric cries.

Tired and frustrated, Marie buried her head in her hands.

Way to traumatize your child, Marie.

Mother of the year.

She hates you.

And with that thought process running through her head, Marie leaned against her daughter's bed and began to cry.

Chapter 16

Frankie and Levi turned onto Arlington Road from Cherry Street. Other than a few grumblings about Evelyn, they tow of them had mostly been quiet ever since they had left Meyer's Place. The weather was cooling, although the sun was still bright in a cloudless sky. The mood of the day seemed to contrast the thoughts flowing through Frankie's mind.

He had been thinking about whether or not it was a good thing to talk to Anna. What would he do if his own grandchildren walked up to his doorstep one day, looking older than he currently was? How would he react? What would he say?

Chances are, he'd be pretty freaked out, and he

assumed Anna was going to be too. He didn't want to do anything that would harm her or cause any repercussions into the future.

Evelyn's nagging voice rang in his head, which was annoying.

"So this is the same house as the one you live in, huh?" Levi's voice broke into Frankie's thoughts.

It wasn't until he looked up that he realized he had stopped in front of the house. It was like second nature, walking the same number of steps from the end of the street to the front walk of this house. No matter the differences in the surroundings from this time to the one he was used to, his body—his soul—knew where his home was. Always.

"Just about. There have been some changes over the years, but it's more or less the same." Frankie sucked in a deep breath and tried to gain the courage to cross the street and knock on the door. For whatever reason, the idea of actually going inside the house unnerved him. Maybe it was the fear of messing up things for the future. Or maybe it was the fear that he would never see his own version of this house again. The way he had always remembered it. With his daughters. He wasn't sure how he'd feel stepping back into the house and being overwhelmed with the memories. And the regrets.

"Any idea how you're going to start the conversation?" Levi asked.

"No," he replied with a dry voice. He cleared his throat. "I might just try to play it off that I'm a fellow witch who is concerned about her."

"And you think that'll work?"

"If I can be convincing enough, sure." Frankie sized up the house and took in another deep breath.

"Nervous?"

"A little. Can you keep a secret?" He looked down at his friend.

"Um…maybe. What is it?"

"My family has this book of magic," Frankie started. "It was first created a long time ago by some of our ancestors and has been passed down through generations. It contains every bit of knowledge related to the supernatural that our family has encountered. And it continues to grow. It's called *The Art of Magic*."

"Okay…"

"I originally came here this morning because I was going to try to sneak inside and get a spell from it," Frankie confessed. "I wanted to see if there was a way that I could transport myself back to my time without Zanabar."

Levi nodded. "Ah. I see. That's why Evelyn was mad at you."

"I didn't tell her about that part. And I don't want you to either." Frankie turned back to the house. "But I am hoping that Anna can help me get back to my time."

"Wait a minute. That would involve you telling her who you are and where—or rather, *when*—you're from."

Frankie nodded. "Mm-hmm."

"And isn't that *exactly* what Evelyn told you not to do?"

"Evelyn doesn't understand."

"What's there not to understand about this? If you tell too many people from the past about the future, that's bad. There's no way around it. Sounds like Evelyn has a right to be mad at you."

"Unless the person in the past you're telling about the future won't *be* in the future."

Frankie could feel Levi's eyes on him. "What are you saying?"

"My grandmother died young. My father doesn't even remember her."

"Oh."

Frankie pointed to the house across the street. "So this woman who I'm about to meet for the first time only has a little over a year left to live. If I'm going to tell the truth to anyone in my family, she's the one to tell."

"But if you're successful in using this spell with her," Levi started, "and you go back to your time, then who will be here to stop Lady Luck?"

Frankie clenched his jaw as he stared at the house. "I don't know."

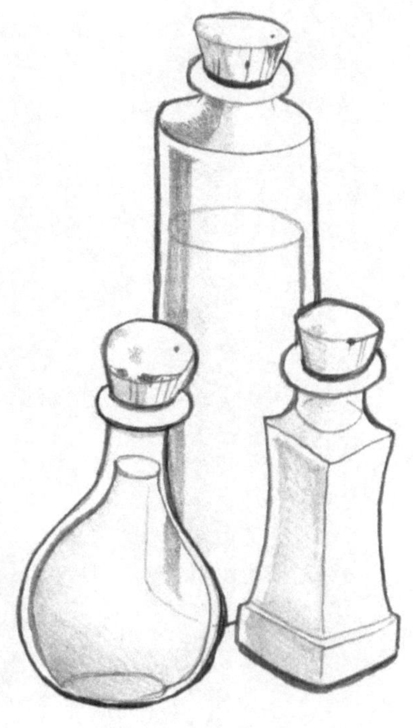

Chapter 17

Evelyn sat at her usual table in the speakeasy with a cigarette in one hand and a drink on the table in front of her. She sat with her eyes closed, focusing, concentrating, meditating. She reached into the depths of her soul to access her true power to call up a vision.

Opening her eyes just briefly, she set her cigarette on the edge of the ash tray and reached for the empty glass on the table. It was the same one Lady Luck had been drinking from when she made her last deal here only an hour ago. That was all that Evelyn had to concentrate on to call up a vision.

Even though she had been trying to call a vision, the

first one took her by surprise, hitting her consciousness just as quickly as something jumping out at her.

Frankie sat in a house—presumably Anna's—and talked with her. The front door opened and Lady Luck walked in. Words were shared, but in this particular vision, Evelyn couldn't make out exactly what was being said.

Even so, she could tell that they were harsh words being exchanged between Lady Luck and Frankie—*Where is Levi?* she wondered idly—while Anna sat on the couch, a demur expression on her face. She sat quietly on the couch, averting her eyes to her two guests.

Swirling her hands in the air in front of her, Lady Luck turned them palms-out toward Frankie, sending a streak of light directly at him. Frankie's eyes showed his surprise as the light struck him.

Just as quickly as the vision came, it was suddenly gone. Evelyn put a hand over her racing heart in an effort to calm herself.

What exactly had she seen? Lady Luck was going to put some sort of spell on Frankie, but what was it? Did she have the power to kill? Or just crank up the bad luck until something so strange happened that death was imminent? And was that the present or the future? Maybe even the past? Had enough time passed for Frankie and Levi to get up to Arlington and get into

Anna's house to talk to her? And where was Levi in that vision?

She couldn't remember when exactly they had left, but she wasn't going to wait any longer.

Evelyn scooted around the table, but stopped as another vision struck her.

This time, she saw Lady Luck confronting an unfamiliar man in a small apartment. One Evelyn hadn't ever seen before.

Once again, there were words exchanged in the vision, but Evelyn couldn't hear them. She could only witness the motions of the two people she was seeing.

Finally, Lady Luck exited the apartment and the man opened a window and stepped out onto a metal fire escape and lit up a cigarette. As he shifted his weight onto the railing, the supports below gave way and the whole fire escape crashed down to the ground, bringing the man down with it.

When Evelyn snapped out of her vision, she let out an involuntary yelp at having seen a man fall to her death in her vision. She put her hand to her heart again, which was racing faster this time.

At the door leading upstairs, Sid took notice of Evelyn's reaction. He was a big, stocky man but he had a soft spot for Evelyn. He was always very protective of her, eyeing her from across the room whenever she performed readings on people. On more than one occasion, he had forcefully asked drunk men to leave when they raised their voice to Evelyn after hearing a reading they didn't like. This time was no different. He crossed the room quickly, coming to Evelyn's side and dropping to one knee in front of her. He took her dainty hand in his big, calloused one. "Are you okay?"

She reached for her cigarette and took several puffs to help calm herself down. Then she nodded. "Yes. I'll be okay." She smiled at him sweetly, then planted a kiss on his cheek. "I just had a vision. A bad one."

Everyone in the speakeasy knew that Evelyn read people's fortunes. Not everyone believed that she *wasn't* a con artist. Whether or not Sid was a believer or not was irrelevant. He respected Evelyn and her way of life too much to ask any questions.

He nodded. "Are you sure you're okay?"

"Um...I'll be okay." Her mind was on her visions. Two separate visions. Two people in need. Lady Luck was in both of them, so they couldn't have happened at the same time. And judging by where both had taken place, she guessed that neither were near each other, which meant that she had time to act. How much, she didn't know.

"Why don't I get you a glass of water?" Sid rose to his feet and took one step toward the bar.

"That won't be necessary," she told him. "I have to run." She downed the contents of her highball cocktail and winced as it burned on its way down. Then she got to her feet and went to the stairs. "Thank you for your concern. But I have to run."

Evelyn could feel Sid's eyes on her—and everyone else in the bar—so she made sure to exit the room with the same level of grace that she always carried herself with. But inside she was worrying, wondering if she was going to make it to her friends in time to stop whatever she had seen in her vision.

Time was not on her side.

The girls look exhausted and the house is a mess."

Marie unscrewed a bottle of ibuprofen and deposited two pills into her palm. She poured a glass of water, downed the pills and took a swig. "It's been a long day."

"How'd the doctor appointments go?"

She glared at him. "Samantha has an ear infection but she refuses to take her meds for it. I even tackled her to the ground, but she knocked it out of my hand." She sighed. "There's a mess in her room from that. She's been a terror all day and neither of them will go down for a nap, so I gave up trying to fight with them."

Frankie walked up and pulled her into a hug. "I'm sorry you had such a rough day."

As Marie leaned into him, she did feel a little better. If for nothing else than for the sole relief of having a co-pilot in the house of madness surrounding them.

"Give it back!" Kathy cried from the other room.

Samantha came running in and took refuge behind the kitchen island. Kathy chased after her.

Frankie kissed the top of his wife's head. "Why don't you go lay down? I'll wrangle these rugrats and get dinner ready."

Marie muttered a thanks and then started to leave. In the doorway, she turned and said, "Oh, Samantha's medicine is right there on the table. See if you can get her to take it. Three drops in the ear, three times a day. If not, we can try again in the morning."

"No!" Samantha crossed her arms and stomped her foot. "I'm not going to take it."

Frankie took the bottle and knelt down beside her. "I know it probably feels weird in your ear, but it'll help you feel better."

"I tried that," Marie said.

"How about this, then?" Frankie asked Samantha. "There's an extra cookie with your name on it if you take your medicine. You might not like it, but the cookie will help you forget about it."

Samantha thought it over and then said, "Okay."

Marie watched in amazement as Samantha willingly sat still for Frankie to drop the medicine in her ear, then extended her hand for a chocolate chip cookie. Kathy, of course, wanted a cookie as well.

"That's what I tried—" Marie stopped her complaining. Whatever worked. As long as Samantha got the medication in her body, what difference did it make if it was Mom or Dad who gave it to her?

Frankie looked at his wife and shrugged as he reached for a bag of cookies from the cupboard.

I can't even do my job as a mother right, Marie thought to herself. *All day these girls haven't been listening to me. In five minute, Frankie starts to get this place in order.*

She cast another look at her husband and how well

he rounded the girls up, even after working a long day himself. He got them involved with dinner, asking them what they wanted, giving them simple jobs to keep them occupied, all while maintaining a level head. Something she hadn't been able to accomplish all day. And not for lack of trying.

Back in the living room, Marie picked up a couple toys, but stopped.

What's the point? she thought. *They obviously don't need me.*

Chapter 19

From the moment Frankie stepped into his grandmother's house, he felt almost disoriented. It was an odd sensation to be in a house that felt so familiar to him and yet still so foreign. The general layout was more or less the same. The biggest difference was that without the kitchen addition, the room that Frankie knew as the dining room also had a small kitchen at the back.

But there were other things that were different too. While Frankie had always been proud of the fact that a lot of the furniture in his house was very old, the ones he saw in this house were different from what he remembered. Likewise, some of the wallpaper choices had changed over the years. Even some of the finer architectural details tucked away in the corners of the house were missing.

"It's such a nice day, why don't we sit in the sunroom?" Anna ushered them through the living room and into a room with full windows overlooking the landscaped yard. One hand rested on her large belly. "Would you like some tea?"

Levi looked to Frankie, then to Anna. "Yeah, that would be nice."

"Of course. I'll be right back." She smiled at them and then disappeared through the door to the kitchen.

"Nervous?"

Frankie shook his head. "No."

"You might want to tell that to your knee." Levi pointed to Frankie's bouncing leg.

Immediately, he stopped. "I just don't want to say the wrong thing. We need to approach this delicately."

"Well, she let us in the door after we only asked her to talk, so I think she's pretty open to anything."

"That's just because people in this time are so trusting."

That seemed to confuse Levi. "Why shouldn't we be? Are there, like, murders and home invasions all the time in 1984?"

Frankie raised his eyebrows. "You'd be surprised."

"Here we are." Anna came back with a large tray with a tea set. The tray shook as she struggled with its weight.

Frankie shot to his feet. "Here, let me help you with that." He took it from her and set it on the small wicker table beside the furniture.

Anna rested one hand on her belly and reached for the back of the chair with her other as she sat down. "Oof. Thank you for helping, dear. I'm not as agile as I usually am. The baby has been growing like a weed lately!" She gestured to the tray. "Please, help yourselves!"

Both Frankie and Levi reached for their cups, doctoring them up to their liking. Anna did the same, with effort to reach around her belly, and then sat back in her chair.

"So, what brings you boys out? You said your names were Frankie and…?"

"Levi," he said.

"Ah, that's right!" She sipped her tea and studied Frankie. "You look familiar. Have we met before?"

"No, we haven't." Frankie kept it firm, but polite.

"Are you sure? I feel like I know you or I've seen you somewhere. I just can't place it." She pinched her chin as she looked, then sat back and said, "You know what? You look just like my husband, William Walker. He goes by Will most of the time. Maybe you've met him?"

"Uh, well…" he started before Levi cut in.

"Frankie's new to town. Just got here last month, so he doesn't really know anyone. But, you know, we don't want to take up too much of your time. We were just hoping to talk to you about something."

"Oh? I don't see what there is to talk about if we've never met. Although, I do enjoy the company."

"We need to talk about Lady Luck," Frankie said plainly. No sense in hiding it or trying to cover it up.

"Oh." Her tone was flat. Deflated. She set her tea down on the table beside her and folded her hands over her belly. "And how would you two know about her?"

"We've been tracking her," Frankie said. "She's hurting people. Did you see in the paper that Charles Bennett died? That was at her hands."

Anna scoffed and looked away.

Frankie leaned in close and added another bomb: "I know you're a witch. I'm one too."

Propping herself up with both hands on the arms of the chair, Anna propelled herself to her feet and walked to the window. She was quiet, although she hadn't asked them to leave, so Frankie decided to let the silence last while she absorbed everything he had said.

Finally, she spoke up. "Are you related to my husband somehow?"

Again with that. "I'm really just here to talk about Lady Luck."

She turned back to face him. "It's just that, you look so strikingly familiar. So much like William."

"Did you make a deal with Lady Luck?" He thought that ignoring her comments would be the best way to steer the conversation away from her recognition of him.

The only thing was, Frankie hadn't counted on his grandmother being so stubborn. And it was a little disorienting to call her his grandmother when, in this time, she was so much *younger* than him.

Anna crossed her arms over her belly. "I'll answer your question only after you've answered mine."

Frankie sighed and glanced back at Levi, who didn't seem to have any other answers. Turning back to Anna, he admitted, "Yes, I'm a relative."

The answer, however, didn't satisfy Anna. She continued to eye Frankie skeptically. She shook her head slightly. "Yes, you are. But…you're not a cousin or a brother. You're…a descendant."

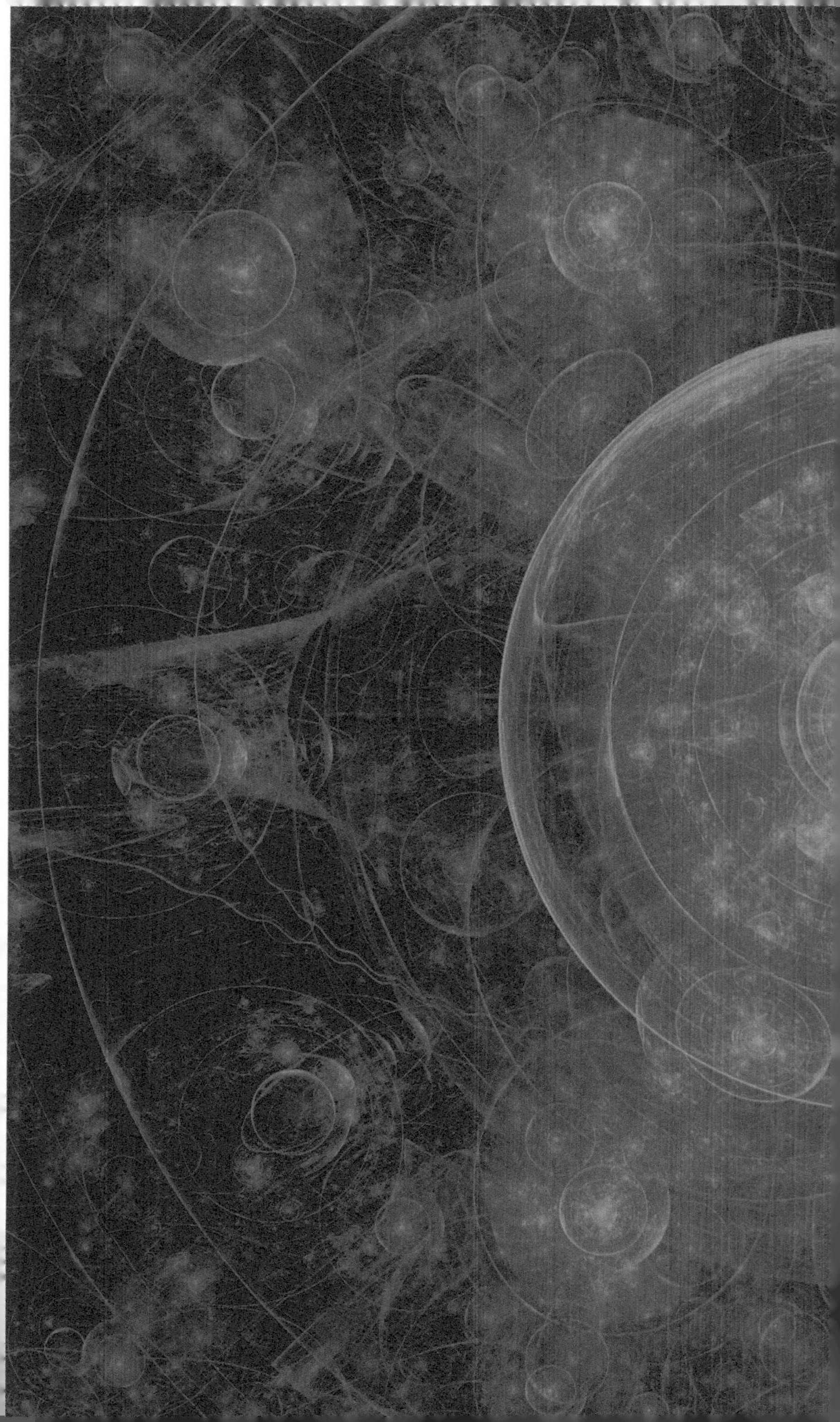

Chapter 20

- Wednesday, September 17, 1924 -

The journey out of the city was not an easy one for Evelyn. Especially after having made the same journey earlier that morning. But still, the oracle pressed on, driven by the events played out in her vision.

The trolley only went to 26th Street, so the rest of the way, along Peach Street, Evelyn had to travel on foot. The dust from the road kicked up, as the city still hadn't paved the roads quite that far south yet. But development was happening in the area. There were some buildings, a few houses, but mostly there were only the early starts to streets and stakes marking out building lots. Many other lots had signs in the ground advertising that those lots were available for sale.

Lucky by Magic

On the corner of Peach and Richley, there was a nearly-barren field where future houses would likely be. For the moment, however, it was mostly empty. Except for Lady Luck walking up the first path that would soon become Richley Street.

Her white ensemble was in stark contrast to the empty, dusty landscape. But still, no dirt seemed to settle on her, and the afternoon sun apparently didn't have any effect on her, either.

"Well, well, well," Lady Luck said with a smile. "Fancy meeting you here."

Evelyn took a defensive stance, but the truth was, she was practically in the middle of nowhere. There were no hiding places and no one around to interfere if Lady Luck decided to strike.

Then again, with nothing around, that meant that Evelyn was safe from whatever bad luck Lady Luck might direct at her.

"Where do you think you're going?" Lady Luck asked.

"I had a vision that you were going to hurt Frankie." She also remembered that she hadn't seen Levi in that vision and she suddenly grew concerned that something had already happened to him.

Lady Luck laughed. "Is that right? Well, from what little I understand about the power of foresight, I know that it's largely a guessing game. One that is heavily influenced by…luck."

The oracle could feel her heart beat faster. "What have you done?"

She smirked. "Don't you worry about a thing. I've simply turned the tables back in my favor."

"Meaning?"

"Meaning I can't have you and your friends undoing my work. I had to take certain liberties to ensure my success."

"I swear, if you've hurt them—"

"Hasn't this already been settled?" Lady Luck asked. "I don't hurt people. I merely adjust their luck. And in this case, that's all I've done. Now, if you'll excuse me, I have other business to attend to." She walked toward Evelyn and offered her a wave as she passed by.

"We're going to stop you," Evelyn promised as she watched the woman in white leave. "You can't keep doing this."

Lady Luck didn't respond. She continued down Peach Street, deeper into the heart of the city.

CHAPTER 21

Marie was quiet the whole way to the restaurant. When Frankie had first suggested that they have a night out with just the two of them, she liked the idea. The thought was that spending some time away from the girls would help her feel more like herself. Adult conversation without having to worry about the kids' entertainment.

But she felt nothing but apathy as she said goodnight to the girls when they dropped them off at James and Helen's house. And that scared her. She had never had issues with attachment before. Never had any kind of postpartum depression with either girls. Now, all of a sudden, she felt numb.

Of course, she felt numb to nearly everything lately. The only thing that seemed to cheer her up was when the waiter set a basket of bread on the table while he listed off the specials.

It took every ounce of self-control for Marie to wait for him to leave before diving into the bread.

"Nice place," Frankie murmured as he looked over the menu. "We haven't been here since our first wedding anniversary. You remember that?"

Marie nodded and gorged herself on the bread. It was delicious. And filling. The salty garlic butter that was smeared liberally over the top of each one. The warm, soft inside. She couldn't seem to get enough. She didn't care how much she ate.

"Are you going to save room for your meal?" Frankie asked.

"Huh?" Marie realized that she was reaching for the last piece of bread. Guilty, she pushed it toward her husband, who hadn't had any yet. "Oh. Sorry."

"That's okay. If you want it, you can have it."

The look on his face said otherwise. Suddenly, Marie felt very self-conscious.

"What's been going on with you?" Frankie asked. "You haven't been yourself for a couple of days now."

Marie shrugged and glanced down at her own menu, not really reading it. "I've just been feeling off, that's all."

"Is it the girls? Seems like they've been extra tough this week."

She shrugged, not wanting to blame her mood on her daughters, but not having any other answer.

Silence filled the table again as they both turned to their menus. The waiter came and took their orders. Even after he left, neither of them seemed to have anything to talk about.

The awkward silence was lifted only when their food finally arrived. Marie grabbed her silverware before the plate was even set in front of her and she dove in before the waiter had even left the table.

"Hungry?" Frankie asked.

She nodded, not wanting to slow down to speak. Nothing felt as good lately as this meal tasted. She dug into her pasta and slurped up the spaghetti noodles that were coated in Alfredo sauce. A heavy meal, but one that made her feel *something* for the first time in a while.

"Easy, honey, it's not going anywhere," Frankie warned from across the table. "We can stay as long as we need to. The girls are spending the night at my parents'. It's just me and you tonight."

Marie scarfed down the rest of her meal before Frankie was even done with half of his. She reached for the dessert menu in the center of the table and looked at the options. "I want something sweet."

"You finished already?" His eyes were wide with surprise, but when he caught her looking at him, his expression turned to concern. "These are large plates, honey. Are you sure you're still hungry?"

"You're not?"

Frankie pushed his plate away from him. "No, I'm full."

"Can I finish it?"

He eyed her, but lifted his plate and handed it to her. "Knock yourself out. Just be careful you don't make yourself sick."

"I'll be fine."

Marie reached for his plate and devoured the rest of Frankie's meal. She was licking the fork clean when the waiter came over.

"Will that be all for tonight?" The waiter kept his eyes locked on Frankie. A silent plea to take the check and leave so that Marie's strange behavior would no longer upset the other customers.

"Yeah, you can bring the check." With the waiter gone, Frankie looked across the table at his wife. She was now sitting quietly, staring at the tablecloth. No expression on her face whatsoever.

"Are you okay?"

"I'm fine. Do you want to stop for ice cream on the way home?"

Frankie felt his stomach pressing against the waistband of his pants. "I'm really full. I think we have a carton at home, if you wanted some there."

Marie's face fell. "Oh. Okay."

He was about to question her further, but the waiter returned with the check.

"Here you are, sir."

"Thank you." Frankie glanced at the amount and set a fifty dollar bill in the check presenter. That would be enough to cover their meals and the tip. "Are you ready?"

Marie stood and extended her hand out to him. "Can I drive?"

It was the most interest she had shown in anything all day. Granted, Frankie thought that she'd use her position behind the wheel to stop at an ice cream place on the way home. But if it brought a smile to her face, he wouldn't object to her indulgence.

He fished the keys out of his pocket and handed them to her as they made their way outside. "Sure."

Once Marie got behind the wheel, though, Frankie regretted handing her the keys. Not only did she fly out of the parking lot and cut off two cars in the process, but she ran almost every red light and raced at top speeds.

"Marie, slow down." Frankie braced himself against the seat, grabbed the handle above the door to help ground himself. "Watch out for that—you almost hit him!" The car raced by a man in the crosswalk. Frankie jerked around to make sure he was okay.

Marie glanced in the rearview mirror. "He's fine."

"Why are you going so fast?"

"What's the harm? Everyone's fine."

"Just slow down."

The next turn forced her to slow, but then she raced back up to top speed as quickly as she could, whipping around a turning car and nearly colliding with an oncoming one. It slammed on its horn and waved a middle finger in her direction.

Frankie wondered if a police officer would pull them over. Having to plead guilty to a speeding ticket was the last thing they needed, but maybe it would knock some sense into his wife.

Soon, they were pulling into their driveway and mercifully coming to a stop.

"Honey, what the hell was that?" Frankie demanded.

Marie ignored him and got out of the car.

"That was completely reckless!" He chased after her up the front steps toward the door.

"We're fine," she murmured. "I got us home, didn't I?"

Frankie let the argument slide. This was their night alone. He wanted to spend it with his wife. Preferably, not mad at each other.

Inside, Marie kicked off her shoes by the door and started toward the stairs.

"Do you want to watch a movie?" Frankie asked in a softer tone. "Or we could pour some wine. Just sit and relax. Maybe talk or something."

"I'm tired." She walked up the stairs. "I'm going to bed."

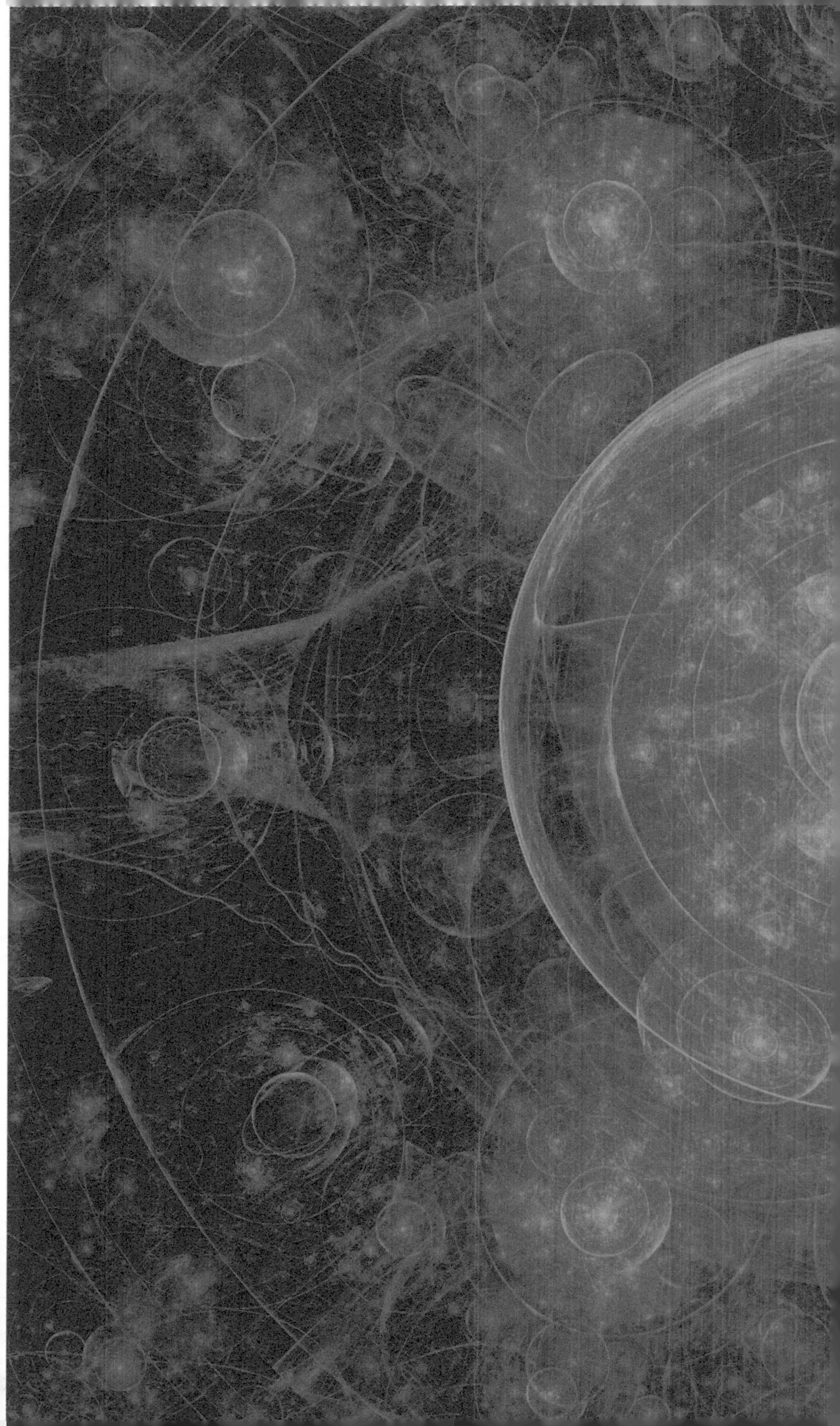

CHAPTER 22

Frankie and Levi exchanged looks.

"Why would you say that I'm a descendant?"

"Well, the resemblance is the biggest indicator." Anna reached for her teacup and held it, but didn't take a sip. "Our family is quite small, so I feel as though I've met everyone on both mine and my husband's side. Then there's the fact that you seemed to be familiar with this house. Don't think I didn't notice the way you studied everything as you walked in."

Frankie kicked himself for being so transparent. Then again, this was personal for him. It hit home in a way that nothing else ever had before.

"And then there was the fact that you were watching

the house earlier this morning," Anna finished. "At first I thought maybe you wanted to do me harm, so I cast a protection spell after you left. The fact that you're sitting here now and haven't been incinerated into flames is a good indicator that you can be trusted."

Levi leaned toward Frankie. "She doesn't mess around."

Frankie ignored him. "I was only watching this house so I could warn you about Lady Luck."

"Is that so? Because the look on your eye when you saw her leave this morning seemed to me like surprise, not concern." Anna took a sip. "And if you truly came here this morning to warn me about Lady Luck, then why wouldn't you have knocked on my door right after she left? Instead, you made a second venture out of the city to see me."

Levi shifted uncomfortably beside Frankie. Neither of them had any explanation for the way Anna had just called them out like that.

She casually took another sip of her tea. "What time period are you from?"

Frankie took a deep breath, ready to divulge his secret, but Levi spoke up before he could.

"That's not really necessary, is it?" he asked.

"It's okay," Frankie told him. "She has a right to know." He looked back to Anna. "I'm from 1984."

She nodded. "Sixty years from now. So that would make you…my grandson?"

Frankie nodded.

"That would explain the resemblance, then."

"That's all I can tell you, though," Frankie said. "I can't reveal too much, or I could risk altering my future."

"Yes, that would be unfortunate," she murmured, lost in thought.

"I only came here to warn you about Lady Luck. That part is true. Do you realize what you've signed up for? The fate that you've subjected yourself to?" He realized his words sounded accusatory, so he added, "She can be manipulative."

Anna retook her seat and stared blankly at the floor. "I know she can. And I know what she does, and how she gets payment. But I had no other choice."

"We've discovered that Lady Luck has been using her power to kill people," Levi said, matching Anna's soft tone. "We don't want to see that happen to you."

This caught her attention. "No. She's not killing them. She's only making deals with them."

"And when the deal is over, people die," Frankie said. "Look at Charles Bennett."

"That was suicide."

"Because he was so worried about what would happen when his luck changed," Frankie said. "He committed suicide so his wife wouldn't have to go through the turmoil of watching everything they had gained in the last year taken away from them."

"I'm not worried about it," Anna said. "I'm a witch. I can handle myself."

"If that were true, then why would you make the deal with her to begin with?" Frankie asked.

Levi nudged him, a sign that Frankie had gone too far. But he was getting frustrated at his grandmother for not giving any credence to his warning.

"What was so important that made you turn to Lady Luck anyway?" he asked in a kinder voice. "What made you want to risk your life for some temporary good luck?"

"It's personal."

"I may be some stranger who just walked up to your door, but I'm your grandson, whether you believe it or not," he said. "Anything that happens to you is a direct link to me and my life in the future. If you die, then so do I. Personal or not, you need to tell me why you made that deal. Please."

She reached for her belly and rubbed it absently. There were tears in her eyes and she struggled to keep the emotion out of her voice. "My baby. Your mother, father? Uncle, aunt?"

"My father." Frankie sat back, surprised. He didn't

know this piece of his history. He wondered if even his father knew.

Anna wiped tears from her eyes. "I've been going to my regular doctor appointments, like I'm supposed to. The doctor seems concerned about the baby's health. He says the heartbeat is weak. And I've been very tired lately." She shook her head. "He seems to think I won't go full-term. And if I don't go full-term, then the baby has a less likely chance at survival." She sniffled. "I just needed good luck to make sure that both me and my baby survive."

Frankie felt his heart drop. If he had known this is what his grandmother was worried about, maybe he could've come earlier and assured her—simply through his presence—that everything was going to work out okay. At least for the birth. He didn't have to tell her that she wouldn't get to see her son grow old. That was a weight that no mother—no *parent*—should ever have to bear.

It was a reality that Frankie was coming to grips with himself.

"Does childbirth kill me?" She wiped at her eyes.

Frankie shook his head and got down on his knees. He took Anna's hands in his. "No, childbirth won't kill you. But listen, I'm here to tell you that you have nothing to worry about. I mean, that baby is my father. And here

Lucky by Magic

I am, completely healthy, and I'm telling you that my father will live a happy life."

He was careful about the words he used. Both of his parents had died relatively young. Slipping and letting Anna know that would only add to her stress—and her assurance that she had made the right choice in going to Lady Luck.

"Maybe your father only survived *because* I made the deal with Lady Luck," Anna said. "Maybe this was a part of our history all along, but you didn't know it."

Valid point, but Frankie wasn't willing to believe it.

"You just have to trust me." Frankie squeezed her hands. "Bad luck is not how you die."

Anna sucked in a shuddering breath and nodded. "Okay. Okay. So the deal is bad. But it's already been made. Now what can we do?"

Frankie smiled. "We're going to help."

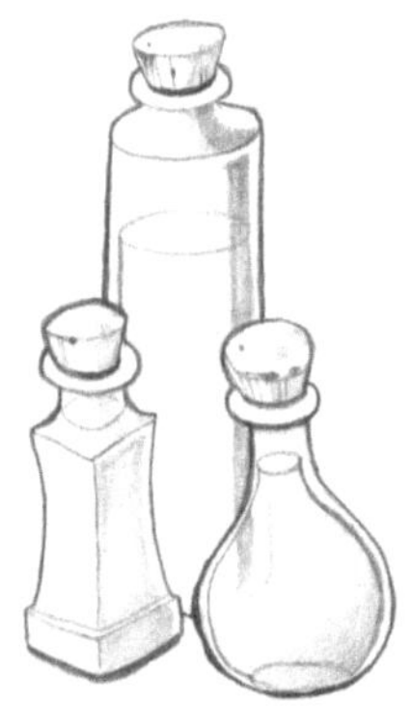

CHAPTER 23

Oddly enough, the upstairs foyer of Anna's house looked nearly identical to the way that Frankie remembered it from his time. All of the intricate woodwork that seemed to be missing on the first floor was firmly in place on the second. Even some of the furniture remained in the same place that it had in Frankie's time, which begged the question: when was the last time he had moved it? If and when he got back to his time, he would give the full house a deep clean. He couldn't remember the last time he did that.

Anna didn't notice any of the things that caught her grandson's attention. She went straight to a table with ornate, decoratively carved legs that was tucked into the space between two of the bedrooms. On it sat the magic book out in the open, as if there was no threat to it whatsoever.

Perhaps there hadn't ever been one in this time period.

The table looked familiar to Frankie too. In 1984, it had moved to his bedroom and held his 13-inch TV that he used to watch the news in the evenings before going to bed. Ever since his wife had passed, it kept him company in the evenings.

Anna flipped through *The Art of Magic* with an intensity that Frankie recognized in himself in the past. It was determination, as well as a faint recall of a piece of information that was *somewhere* in the loosely-indexed book.

Levi, meanwhile, looked around the foyer. "How come up here has more woodwork and details than downstairs? Wouldn't you want to do downstairs first, to show it off to everyone?"

"My husband is an excellent fine carpenter." Anna continued to flip through the book as she spoke. "Although, he has his doubts about himself, like any perfectionist does. He used this level of the house as a way to practice his skills before he installed any trim downstairs, where more people will see it. If it isn't perfect, he said he doesn't want to be staring at it every day."

"Interesting," Frankie said. "I didn't realize that he installed it *all* himself. That's really cool." He looked around at the familiar features. The ones he had always taken for granted. Now knowing who installed it, he had a newfound appreciation for it all.

She nodded and looked around briefly at her husband's work. "Unfortunately, he hasn't had a lot of time lately to work on it. Ever since we learned that I was expecting, he's been picking up extra shifts and working overtime to help pay for our upcoming expenses. He's been doing fine carpentry for other people's houses in town, which means he doesn't have a lot of time to do our own."

"I was wondering where he was," Frankie admitted. "I figured he was working."

"Yes, he won't be home until after dark, which means that we have plenty of time to take care of this Lady Luck business." She returned to the book and, after a few more pages, pointed to a specific. "Aha! Here we go."

Frankie and Levi stepped on either side of her.

"What is it?" Levi asked.

"It's a potion that could reverse the effects of Lady Luck's magic." She wiggled her nose as she thought. "Hmm. Looks like it's not the best solution. The potion would have to be administered to each of her clients individually."

"It's a start," Frankie said. "How soon do you think we can whip this up?"

Anna's finger trailed over the list of ingredients. "I should have most of these downstairs in the kitchen. What I don't have readily available should be in the garden out back. I try to grow my own herbs so I don't have to keep running into town whenever I need to whip up a potion or two."

"Perfect." Frankie turned to the stairs. "Let's go."

Levi, however, seemed to have his eyes locked on the book.

"Is there something we missed?" Anna asked him.

"No, it's just…" He reached out for the book, but Anna moved her arm over it in a protective manner.

"It's okay," Frankie told her. "He's just curious. He's nonmagical."

Anna eyed him and then turned back to Levi. "Do you have questions?"

"So this has everything you need to know about magic?"

"Well, not *everything*," she said. "But a lot of things. Most things, in fact. Our family has been documenting our magical experiences for a long time."

"The book is even bigger in my time," Frankie added. "Sixty extra years of knowledge."

Levi looked up at him in wonder. "It *grows*?"

He laughed. "Well sure. It's a *magic* book."

"But how does it know when it's time to grow?" Again, he tried to reach for it, but Anna stepped in his way.

She scooped up the large tome and propped it against her body. "That's the thing about magic. You never really know exactly how it works, but it doesn't mean it's not happening. Come on, we can't waste anymore time talking about the book. We have a potion to make and a woman to stop." As she passed by Frankie, she murmured, "I'm going to keep a close eye on him."

Levi looked at Frankie and shrugged. He laughed and patted him on the shoulder.

"We're all very protective of that book," Frankie said. "We'd be lost without it. Don't take it personally."

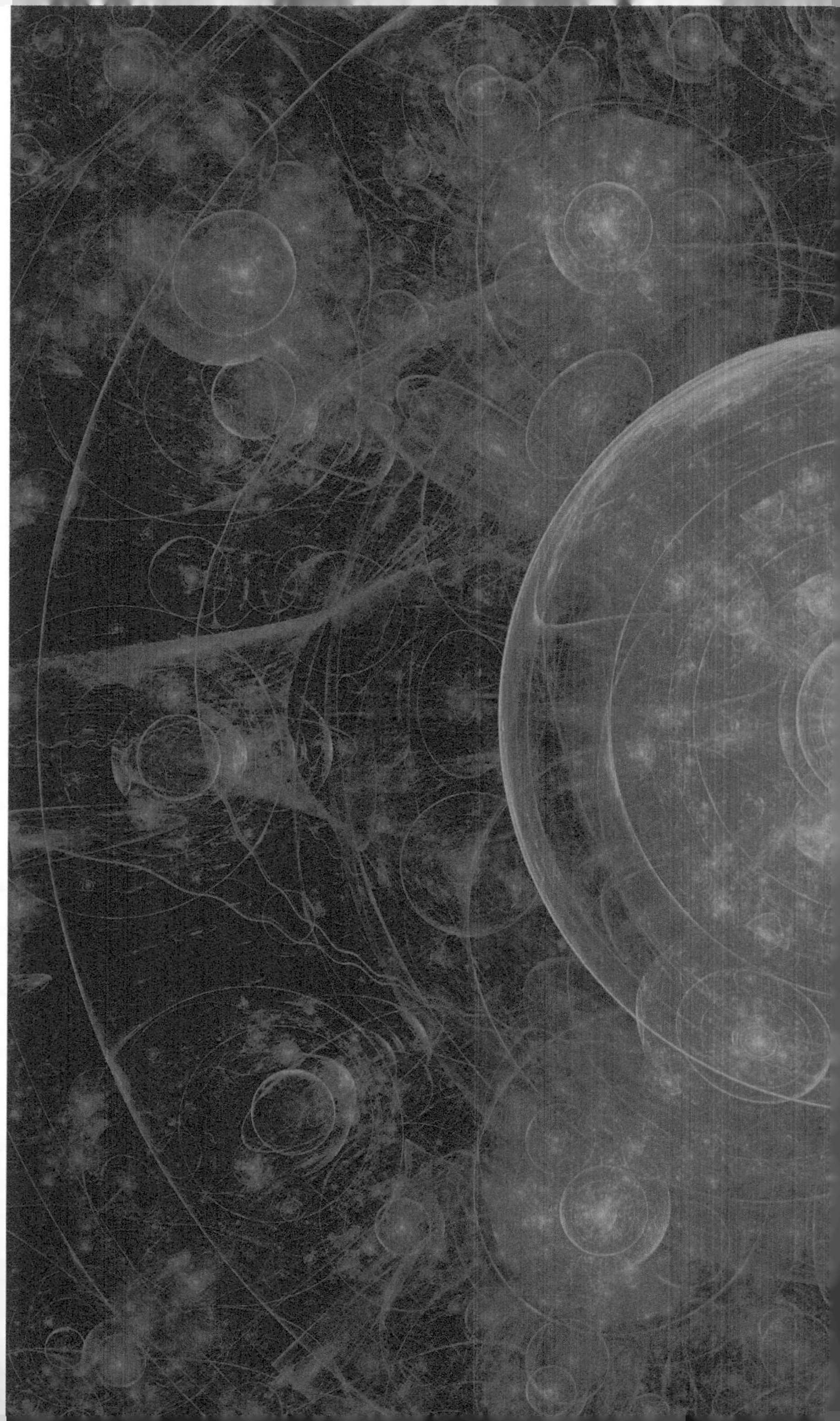

CHAPTER 24

Frankie awoke at the sound of his alarm. What he had thought would be a nice relaxing morning without the girls had been ruined after his disastrous date night with his wife the night before.

He rose from the bed and stretched, then grabbed the pair of jeans that hung over the back of a chair in the corner and pulled them on. He considered waking Marie, but after the disaster the previous night had been, he didn't want to talk to her. Besides, she had said she hadn't been feeling well, so getting more rest was probably in her best interest.

After stopping off at the bathroom, he went down to the kitchen to start the coffee. As he reached for a box of cereal from the cupboard, it hit him: the silence.

Sure, he was used to his quiet mornings before work, but this was different. He didn't hear Marie moving around upstairs. Didn't have the anticipation of getting ready before the girls got up.

Frankie wasn't sure that he liked the quiet. The chaos of having two small kids in the house became too much sometimes, but he was realizing that the noise was actually comforting.

After breakfast, Frankie went back upstairs to shower. The time alone allowed him to think over everything that had happened between him and his wife the night before and the part he played in the bad date.

By the time he turned off the water, he decided to apologize to her and support her. She was clearly going through a hard time. He needed to be there for her and support her through it.

He returned to their bedroom to dress, then went over to Marie's side of the bed and gently shook her shoulder.

"Honey," he said in a soft tone.

Marie groaned and then rolled onto her back. She squinted her eyes as she looked up at him "Huh?"

"Hey, I'm leaving in a few minutes for work, but I just wanted to remind you to pick up the kids from my parents' house this morning."

She stared at the floor, not acknowledging him.

"Do you want me to see if they could keep the kids for the day so you can have a day off?"

Marie gently shook her head, but didn't say anything else.

Frankie smirked. "Do you need a minute to wake up?"

She didn't say anything.

He took her hands and smiled. "Honey?"

"Hmm?"

"Are you still asleep?"

She stared off into space for a minute and then shook her head, as if to clear the cobwebs. "Uh, yeah. I guess so."

The look on her face when she met his eyes concerned him. This wasn't Marie being tired. This was something else entirely.

Then another thought occurred to him: since when did Marie ever sleep in? But then, without the girls, what point was there to wake up early with him if she didn't need to get the girls up and ready too? Sure, she had to go pick them up, but that wouldn't be until nine or ten. She had time to sleep in and enjoy her slow morning.

"Did you hear me about the kids?"

Marie nodded. "Yes. You told me to pick them up from your parents'."

"Right." He studied her. "Are you okay?"

Her eyes met his, not really seeing him. Finally, after another few seconds, she nodded and smiled. "Yes, I'm fine."

Frankie eyed her, not believing that she was perfectly okay. But he wanted to be supportive and give her space, which is what she clearly wanted. "Okay. Then I'm going to head out here shortly. Are you getting up or are you sleeping in a little longer?"

"I might lay around here a little bit longer. It's still early yet."

He nodded. "Okay. Just don't forget Samantha and Kathy."

"I won't. Now, go." She smiled at him, but something about it didn't sit well with Frankie. "You have a job to get to."

He leaned in and kissed his wife. "I love you."

She fussed with the blankets as she got comfortable again. "You too."

CHAPTER 25

Evelyn coughed as wind blew dirt and dust from the road into her face. With her premonition in mind, she marched on. The side of the road was in mid-construction, making it even more treacherous to walk along than if it had simply been left alone.

There were construction materials laying about, trenches for future utilities, and concrete curbs that stuck out of the ground much higher than usual, compared to the height Evelyn was used to seeing in the city with paved streets.

As she navigated all of that, she also tripped over stones and rocks that had been cast to the side by passing cars on the dirt road. With her next step, Evelyn heard a crunch as her balance was thrown off.

The oracle groaned when she looked down and saw that her heel had broken off the back of her shoe. That's what she got for wearing stilettos on the walk out of the city. She had had no problems navigating the terrain earlier that morning, but now she was cursed with bad luck, thanks to Lady Luck herself.

Evelyn bent over to see if there was any saving her shoe. Just as her attention focused to her feet, she heard a passing car blare its horn at her. She looked up in time to see it heading right toward her. She jumped off of the street and stumbled into the brush that was still overgrown in the building lot off of Cherry Street.

When she finally roused herself from the bush, a cloud of dirt and dust was left in the wake of the passing car.

She got up, hearing the familiar sound of fabric tearing as her dress snagged on the branches from the brush. She reached up and picked a couple of twigs out of her short hair and cast them aside. Then, with a heavy sigh, she continued her walk up Cherry toward Arlington.

Come hell or high water, she was going to make it to Frankie and Levi to warn them about her vision. No amount of bad luck would stop her of that.

It wasn't much longer before she felt a tingle from

an itch on her arms. Then on the back of her neck. Then on her shoulder. Soon, most of her upper body seemed to be itchy.

Must've been something poisonous in the brush, she surmised. *Just add that to the pile of bad luck.*

Evelyn was relieved when she saw the turn for Arlington Road up in the distance. It wouldn't be much longer before her trek was over. She just needed to focus and keep her eyes open for anything else that could accidentally—or intentionally—take her out before she got there. Not only was she fighting against time, but she was also fighting against Lady Luck's magic as well.

You brought this on yourself.

The thought struck her so suddenly and seemed to come out of nowhere that Evelyn quickly brushed it aside in her mind. Or at least she tried.

What are you going to do when you actually reach the guys? You're never much help anyway.

The negative thoughts continued to swirl in her mind. She knew it was the effects of Lady Luck's magic taking hold of her, but at the present moment, it was getting hard to see past that. She wasn't feeling like herself. She felt like a failure.

You're always in the way.

She shook her head. Focused on moving forward.

Lucky by Magic

One step at a time. If she could make it to the guys, then she could—

You're pathetic.

Tears began to spill from Evelyn's eyes, but she pressed on. Whether she knew those words were the result of magic or not, they were still ever-present in her mind. And no matter how much she tried to convince herself otherwise, there was a small part of her that thought that Lady Luck couldn't simply create these feelings of insecurity. They had always existed and had come from somewhere deep inside of Evelyn herself. Maybe from a place that she had simply been denying all along. Maybe the thoughts were simply the truth.

Maybe the world would be better off without me.

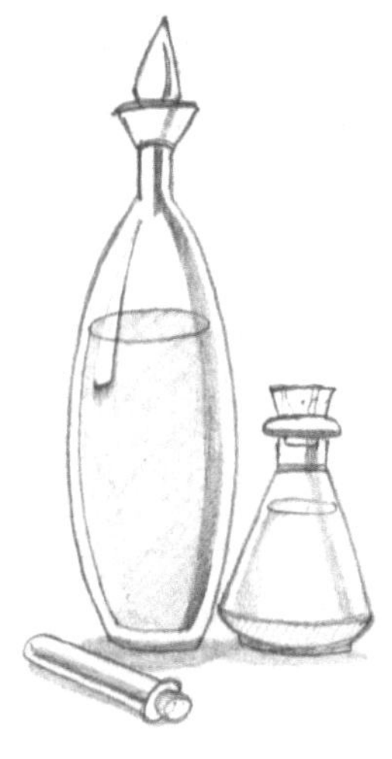

CHAPTER 26

Frankie washed his hands at the sink and watched out the back window as Anna pointed out different plants for Levi to pull from her garden. She stood with one hand on her back to offset her large belly. Occasionally, she would swat at Levi if he was plucking an herb in a way that wasn't to her liking.

From the little gardening Frankie had done in his life, he knew that certain plants were very delicate, and how you handled them determined their success into the future.

With the start of the potion roiling to a boil on the stove, Frankie not needed to worry about occasionally stirring the pot so it didn't burn. He had some time to kill in their absence.

LUCKY BY MAGIC

He went to *The Art of Magic*, which lay open on the kitchen table—the same table that served as the kitchen island in his house in 1984. Turning so he could see Anna and Levi out the back window, he flipped through the magic book quickly in search of a spell or a ritual or something that could help transport him back home.

The trouble was, he didn't even know if such a spell existed. It wasn't something he had ever looked for before in the magic book. Even if he had, there was no guarantee that it would be available in the 1924 edition of the book.

The back door swung open suddenly and Anna stepped back into the kitchen. Frankie's eyes snapped up at her, his hands frozen while the page was mid-turn.

"I need to get that boy some sheers—what are you doing?"

Frankie finished turning the page and shook his head slightly. "Uh—just looking for a way to stop Lady Luck altogether. Since the potion is so limiting."

Anna hooked an eyebrow and stepped to a drawer in the kitchen. "Mm-hmm." She retrieved a pair of sheers and then leaned back against the counter. "Since you're *technically* family, I won't tell you *not* to look at the book, but just know that it makes me uncomfortable."

Frankie took a small step back, carefully removing his hands from the pages of the old tome. "I was just looking. I have the same book at home."

"What were you even looking for? You're older than I am *and* you're from the future. You probably have the contents of this book memorized."

"Not quite." Frankie glanced back at the book, avoiding her scrutiny.

"You're stuck in this time, aren't you?" Anna asked plainly.

He sighed. She was a good witch and someone who clearly didn't let anything get by her. "Yeah."

"Care to elaborate on that tale?"

"Um…well, I mistakenly trusted a sorcerer named Zanabar, who is the one who sent me back here," he started. "I've been stuck in this time for a couple weeks. Unsurprisingly, he double-crossed me. Granted, I didn't necessarily follow through with my end of the bargain, either, but it was for the good of the world."

"Sacrificed yourself to maintain world order?" Anna asked.

He nodded.

"So that's what you were looking for just now?" She tilted her head to the book. "A way to get home?"

Again, he nodded. "Do you know of any way to send me back to my time?"

Anna took a deep breath and readjusted her feet. "Time travel takes immense power. Personally, I have not known anyone who could do it. Not *well*, anyway."

"But it's possibly."

She gave him a sad smile. "Sixty years is a long time. And I hope I don't need to tell you that each generation of magic gets stronger than the one before. Magically speaking, you have more power than I do. And if you haven't found a way, I certainly wouldn't be able to pull it off, either."

Frankie frowned. "That's what I figured."

Anna studied him for a minute. "What I *do* know is that the more witches behind a spell, the stronger the spell becomes. I'd be willing to try to help you get back home. Seems like you have someone special to return to."

"Two special people," he said. "My daughters."

Anna's eyes welled up. "Yes, well, then it's important that we get you back to them. How about we take care of Lady Luck and then we can look into your options for returning home? Sound good?"

Frankie smiled. "Sounds perfect. Thank you."

"This is no guarantee," she warned. "I said I'd *try*. But if it's my *great*-granddaughters you're trying to get back to, then I can't let them down." She turned and looked to the ceiling as she shook her head. "Listen to me. I don't sound like a twenty-year-old woman."

The two of them looked at each other. Frankie felt the urge to give her a hug, but held back. Even though she was his grandmother, at this present moment, she was actually younger than he was. Actually, she was much closer in age to his *daughter* Samantha.

The tender moment came to an abrupt halt, however, when the front door burst open. Evelyn limped in, looking exhausted. Her dress was torn in several places, her hair was a mess, and her skin was red and splotchy.

"Evelyn?" Frankie took a step toward her. "What happened to you?"

"Lady Luck."

CHAPTER 27

"You want to grab lunch from around the corner?" Gary asked when he walked up to Frankie's office at the City of Erie.

"Sure." Frankie patted his pockets and then looked among the clutter on his desk. He took a seat and lifted stacks of papers, plumbing valves, tools, and all kinds of other things that had accumulated on his desk over the course of the morning. "I just need to find my—ah, here it is."

With wallet in hand, Frankie made it to the doorway of his office before he heard his phone ring. He turned back and listened to it ring once, debating on whether to answer it or not.

"Don't do it," Gary said. "You're on your lunch break."

Frankie checked his watch. "Technically it doesn't start for another five minutes."

"You're really going to be a stickler for the time like that?"

"It'll just take a second." He retook his seat and answered the phone. "Frankie Walker, how can I help you?"

"Frankie dear," Helen said on the other end.

"Mom?"

"Yes, honey, I'm sorry to call you at work. Are you busy?"

"I was just about to go to lunch. What's up?"

"Your father and I were wondering when Marie planned on coming by to pick up the kids."

Frankie looked at the clock on the wall. Just about noon. Marie was supposed to pick them up by ten. "She hasn't yet?"

In the background, Samantha and Kathy's bickering could be heard at a distance.

"Not yet. I tried calling the house, but she hasn't picked up. Was she running errands before she came? Maybe she just lost track of time."

Frankie's brow furrowed. "No. Not that I know of. Unless…something *else* came up." His eyes flickered up at Gary, who leaned against the doorframe. Frankie didn't want to say that maybe a demon or something had showed up, but he assumed his mother would get the reference. She had fought off a bad thing or two in her time.

"Yes, well, that's why I thought I'd check in with you first. If you want, we can take a ride over there."

"No, I can go," Frankie said. "If it was…*something else*, I'd rather keep the girls safe with you guys."

"Yes, that would be a good idea. Call me when you get there. The girls are no trouble, but your father and I had lunch plans and we just thought…" She cleared her throat. "If they need to stay here a little longer, that's okay too."

"Thanks. I'll run home and see what Marie's up to and then I'll give you a call."

When he hung up, Gary said, "So no lunch?"

Frankie shook his head. "Sorry. I have to run home and talk to Marie. She was supposed to pick up the kids from my mom's but she hasn't yet."

"Is everything okay?"

"I'm sure it's fine." Frankie pushed it off. "She probably just got busy with something and lost track of the time."

"Maybe."

"I'll take a rain check, though," Frankie said.

Lucky by Magic

"Monday, lunch is on me."

"I'll hold you to it!"

It took another few minutes of digging around his desk for Frankie to find his keys. When he did, he went down into the basement parking garage. Once he was behind the wheel, he navigated out of the garage and pulled out onto West 7th Street, then down to Sassafras Street.

The whole way home, his mind raced with the possibilities of why Marie hadn't picked up the kids. He dissected every word and mannerism that he had seen in Marie since the night before. She hadn't been herself, that much was for sure. So maybe she just needed a day to sleep and rest. But then, why wouldn't she have called his parents and told them as much? Was she afraid that they would look at her as a bad mom for it?

Frankie was happy to put a momentary pause on his invasive thoughts when he pulled up in front of his house. He came around the front of the car and up the front steps. He jangled the keys in an effort to act casually, but his heart was racing and his hands were a little jittery. He just couldn't shake this feeling that something was wrong.

He tried to convince himself as he walked up the front steps to the door that his shaking hands was just low blood sugar. He needed food and his body was telling him it was time to eat.

Somehow, though, he knew it was more than that.

Because, when he walked through the door, nothing could prepare him for the horror that he witnessed. Marie, hanging from the staircase banister, with a bedsheet tied tight around her neck.

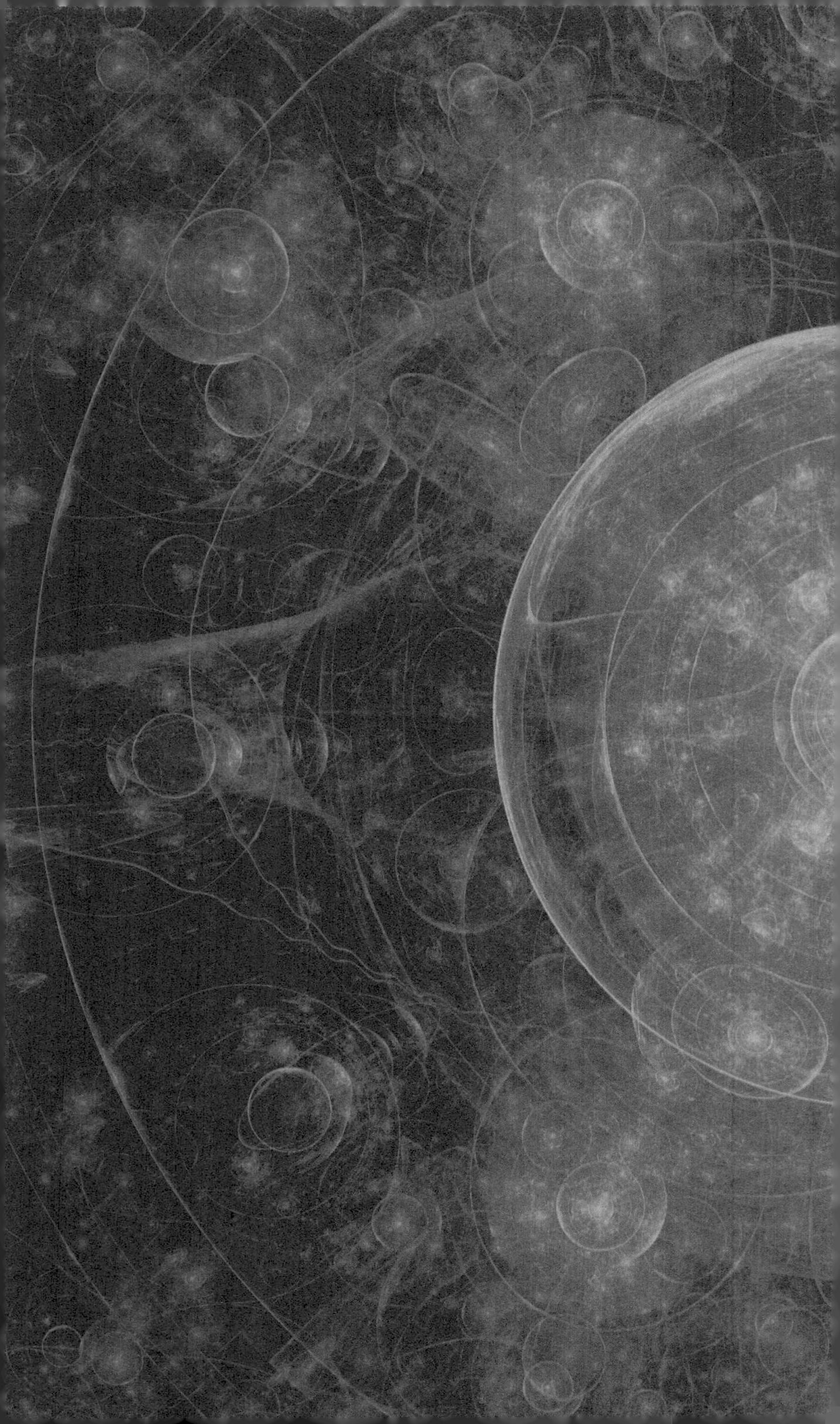

CHAPTER 28

The back door burst open when Levi stepped back inside with a basket full of various ingredients from Anna's garden that they had collected for the potion. He set it on the counter and stepped across the room.

"Evelyn?" he called out.

"Do you know this girl?" Anna asked from the foyer.

Frankie walked over to Evelyn and placed a hand on her shoulder, but she shrugged off his touch.

"No! Don't touch me! I fell in poison ivy or something. I've been itching like crazy."

Anna turned to Levi for clarification.

"She's a friend of ours," he said. "She's a psychic."

"Oracle," Evelyn murmured.

"Let's go sit down." Frankie led Evelyn to the living room, careful not to touch her.

Evelyn took a seat. Levi and Anna followed and stood in the doorway.

"What happened?" Frankie sat in the chair adjacent to her and leaned forward on his knees.

"I was hit with Lady Luck's bad luck." She scratched at her arms. "Are you sure I should be sitting here? I don't want to cause anymore problems. After my run-in with her, I'm radiating bad luck."

"Nonsense, dear," Anna said. "You sit here and rest up. I'll fix you a quick remedy for that itch." She disappeared back into the kitchen.

"Is Lady Luck on her way here, then?" Levi asked. "The potion isn't ready ye—"

"The potion will be fine and so will we." Frankie leaned in close to Evelyn. "Tell us what happened."

"It doesn't matter," she said. "I'm just in the way. I shouldn't have come here. You have enough to worry about." She rose and started toward the door. "I'll just walk home and let you guys take care of this—"

Levi caught her hand before she could reach the front door. "No, you're wrong. We do need you."

"That's not true." She pulled her hand away from his. "You were doing just fine on your own. You already started a potion. Already have a plan. What do you need me for? I'm just in the way."

Levi glanced over at Frankie with wide eyes before turning back to her. "Evelyn, you're the one who figured out that Charles Bennett died at the hands of magic. And you're the one who had the vision of Patrick getting stuck on the railroad tracks—who we were then able to save. We need you."

"It's no use." Frankie walked up from behind him. "She's not really listening. Not in this state. She's convinced that she's not helpful."

Evelyn looked at him with sad eyes. Her shoulders slumped and she wiped at her eyes. "See? Even Frankie recognizes it."

"No, what I see is that a poisonous thought has been planted in your head," he countered with an edge to his voice. "These aren't your own thoughts. They're fake ones, put there to make you believe that you're useless. Lady Luck is behind this. This is the way she *wants* you to feel."

"You think?" Levi asked.

Evelyn stumbled into an end table in the foyer. The vase on the table toppled over and landed on a chair, splattering water into the cushion. It then fell to the floor rolled across the hardwood, where Anna was coming from the kitchen with a steaming pot and a rag over her shoulder. The vase got caught up in her feet and she tripped. She wobbled on her feet, and just as Levi rushed over to prevent her from falling, she dropped to the floor and landed on her butt. Somehow, though, she managed to maintain a tight grip on the pot so only a little spilled onto the floor.

Frankie jumped up and he and Levi both rushed to Anna's side to help her up.

"Are you okay?" Levi asked.

"How's the baby?" Frankie asked.

Back on her feet, Anna reached back for a chair at the kitchen table. "I don't know yet. Give me a minute to get my bearings on what the hell just happened."

"See?" Tears streamed from Evelyn's eyes. "I'm no good."

"Oh, hush up," Anna snapped. She winced as she reached back at her aching behind. "You have bad luck. We all get it sometimes. I, however, happen to have good luck so I think we're evenly matched. In the meantime, the boys and I are working on a fix to your bad luck. Sit down so I can start treating your poison ivy." She turned to Frankie. "I think it's past time that we finish that damn potion."

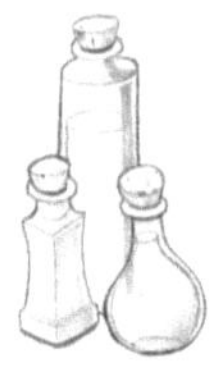

CHAPTER 29

"Just simmer that for a few more minutes and then after it cools, it should be done." Frankie quickly murmured the instructions to Levi as he quietly searched the cupboards in Anna's kitchen.

The women were still sitting in the living room, talking quietly. Not only had Anna treated Evelyn's arms with her home remedy, but she was also likely being a shoulder for Evelyn to cry on during her stint of bad luck. After Anna had snapped at her, the two seemed to come to a mutual understanding and had been locked in quiet conversation ever since.

"What are you doing?" Levi asked Frankie back in the kitchen.

Lucky by Magic

"Looking for a—aha, here we go!" He pulled out a ceramic bowl from a lower cabinet and began filling it at the sink. "I'm going to see if I can find Lady Luck."

"How?"

"This spell—if I'm successful—will let me see where she is and what she's doing," he explained. "Like I'm a fly on the wall."

"You can do that?"

"I'm a witch. I can do anything." Frankie pointed to the kitchen table. "Grab that yellow candle. I need an extra boost with this to counteract her magic."

Levi retrieved it and set it in front of the bowl that Frankie had set on the counter. After lighting the candle, Frankie held his hands over the bowl of water and recited the spell:

> *I call on the strength of my power,*
> *Show Lady Luck's face in the water.*

In the bowl, the image slowly came into focus as the water darkened to illustrate Lady Luck's location. It revealed a duplex house with a wide front porch. Lady Luck walked up to it and knocked on the door. The man who opened it looked shocked—scared—and took off running through the house when he saw her. She followed him through the house, past a family of small children surrounding a dinner table, and out the back door. The man raced into the alleyway behind.

"Can you recognize where that is?" Frankie asked Levi.

"Uh…looks like an alley somewhere."

"I got that much," Frankie said.

"Maybe between—wait, is that a chicken coop?" He leaned his face so close to the bowl that Frankie thought his nose would touch the water and break the spell. "Yeah, he's one of my egg suppliers. That has to be around 12th and German Streets."

"Great, thanks." Frankie blew out the candle, which immediately cut the picture in the bowl, and came around the other side of the table.

"Wait, where do you think you're running off to?"

Frankie pointed to the pot on the stove. "That should only need a couple more minutes, and then you can let it cool."

"Where are you going?"

"Don't tell the girls," Frankie said. "I'll be fine."

"You're not going up against Lady Luck yourself."

"Look what she did to Evelyn. She's a mess. I'm not just going to let Lady Luck torment people's minds like that," Frankie said. "She has to be stopped. And I'm going to be the one to do it."

Before Levi had a chance to protest further, Frankie

slipped out the back door.

Anna came into the kitchen after hearing the back door slam. "What's going on? Where did Frankie go?"

Levi turned off the burner on the stove. "Let's just say, it's a good thing this potion is basically done."

CHAPTER 30

The house was packed for Marie's memorial. Any emotion that Frankie had felt at the sudden loss of his wife was shoved down in order for him to keep a brave face for Samantha and Kathy. Neither of them quite understood where their mother was and Frankie hadn't been able to bring himself to say it out loud. Especially not to them.

Thankfully, his parents had a long conversation with both girls about what had happened and that their mother was gone forever. From what they told him, the girls were coming around to it, although there were a lot of tears. And questions.

Frankie hated that his parents had to be the ones to

have that conversation with them, but it took all of his strength to just keep it together and get all of the arrangements in order.

"I'm so sorry for your loss." Frankie heard those words over and over again, but he barely was able to register who had actually said them. Ever since he had walked in on his wife's body, the days had passed in a blur.

One of the people he did remember, however, was his friend Gary. When he walked in with his own family, the two shook hands and hugged. Gary had been the first one Frankie had called after he had determined that Marie's death was not the result of a supernatural fight.

Suicide.

Gary had mentioned that word when he first showed up on Friday and Frankie had a hard time accepting it. Never in his life did he think Marie was even remotely suicidal. But it made sense if he was only looking at the last several days of her life. She hadn't been herself. She had made comments about how she didn't feel like she was enough. How they'd all be better off without her. Things that she had never struggled with before.

"You need anything, you call me. You got it?" Gary looked at him with wet eyes after they parted.

Frankie nodded and absently glanced up at the staircase.

Gary shook his head and grabbed Frankie by the shoulders to refocus his attention. "Don't keep thinking about it. It'll only torture you."

"I can't help it. Every time I walk by those stairs, I see her…hanging there."

"Look, it's going to take you a long time to get over this—and this is just the beginning—but *don't* let it consume you," Gary warned. "I've seen it happen to guys on the force. They see some terrible shit and they just can't separate it in their mind between the past and where you're heading."

Frankie nodded, more or less because he didn't know how else to react to what Gary was saying. He knew his friend was just trying to help, but it wasn't what he wanted to hear. He wanted answers. An explanation. There had been no suicide note. Just her body.

What was going on in her mind?

"Thanks for coming," he murmured to his friend. "Excuse me."

With his head low to shield the tears that threatened to leak from his eyes, Frankie escaped into the kitchen, which was a safe haven from the other mourners.

Alone, he stood at the kitchen island and took deep breaths to calm all of the feelings that would no doubt break him if he let them surface.

Moments later, he felt his mother hook her arm

around his, then felt his father's pat on his back.

"How are you holding up, dear?" Helen asked.

Frankie tried to swallow the lump in his throat. "Not well. How are the girls?"

"They're…okay. Confused, I think." She shook her head. "They don't truly understand—" She cut herself off as she broke into tears of her own.

James cleared his throat and put his arm around his son. "Your mother and I have been talking." He took a deep breath. "We want you and the girls to move in with us."

Frankie looked at him with surprise.

"With Marie passing—right here in this house, even—we think it would be best if you had a change of scenery," he explained. "And then your mother and I would be right there to help with the girls whenever you need it."

Before his father even finished talking, Frankie had already started to shake his head. "No. I can't. I appreciate the offer, but no."

"Honey," Helen cooed from his other side.

"No. I'm not pulling the girls away from the only home they've ever known—the only home *I've* ever known. Not after what we just lost. We can't change everything." A moment of quiet passed before Frankie added, "Besides, this is a family home. It was built and owned by our family right from the start. I can't just leave it now and break generations of tradition."

"True, but at the end of the day it's just a house," James said. "Helping you and the girls through this is more important than tradition."

That much was true, but Frankie felt a duty to remain in this house. Generations before him had gone through their own personal tragedies. His was not going to break the family cycle. It would only signify that he wasn't nearly as strong as all of the others who came before him. He shook his head. "No, Dad."

"Okay, how about this," Helen countered. "What if your father and I move in here instead?" She looked around her son to her husband.

James raised his eyebrows and shrugged. "That's not a terrible idea."

"That way, the girls stay where they are—they'll need to share a bedroom, but that's not that big of a change for them. And then your father and I will still be here to help."

Frankie thought of Marie and how, only a few days ago, he'd been telling her that she was the glue that kept the household together. She kept it running like a well-oiled machine. He didn't even know where to begin to fill her shoes.

With a nod, he simply said, "Okay."

CHAPTER 31

Frankie was sweating by the time he made it to the alley at 12th and German Streets. He had run most of the way, only slowing at intersections for passing traffic.

And he was just in time, too. The man from the location ritual lay in the middle of the alley, cowering under Lady Luck, who stood over him.

Frankie waved his hand at her and sent her flying back away from the man. The witch rushed up to him and helped him onto his feet.

"Are you okay?"

The man nodded, then his eyes grew large and he started pounding a fist against his chest.

"Can you breathe?"

He shook his head, his eyes going wild.

Frankie remembered that the man had been eating dinner when Lady Luck had arrived at his doorstep. "Great," he said sarcastically. "You're choking." He flicked two fingers toward him and a piece of meat came flying out of the man's mouth and landed on the pavement a few feet away from them.

The man gasped for breath. "Thanks. That was— how the hell did you do that?"

"Don't worry about it right now. You need to get out of here."

"But she's coming to collect on our deal." The man looked around Frankie's shoulder in Lady Luck's direction. She had risen to her feet and was brushing the dirt and mud off of her white outfit, which had been stained.

"And I'm going to squash that deal completely," Frankie assured him. "Now go. She can't hurt you if she can't find you. And be careful! She might've turned your luck bad already."

The man nodded. "Okay. Thank you! Keep an eye on my family."

Frankie looked over to the house. "Go in and take them with you. Keep them all safe. Just for tonight. She shouldn't be a problem anymore after that."

"You know how to stop her?"

"I'm going to try."

The man ran off toward the house.

Frankie turned and saw Lady Luck standing several feet away in the middle of the alley with her arms crossed.

"So now you're just undoing all of my deals, is that it?" she asked. "I make arrangements that everyone agrees to. *Someone* is going to have to pay for them."

"Is that how you justify trying to get Evelyn to kill herself?"

"Suicide? Who mentioned that?"

"I know what you were trying to do." Frankie gritted his teeth. "That line of thinking that you put in her head never leads anywhere good."

Lady Luck chuckled. "Well, if she's feeling bad about herself, then maybe—"

The anger overtook Frankie and he charged at her. For a moment, he saw the look of surprise on her face, but then she regained her composure and simply adjusted her stance over several feet. Frankie made his own adjustments, but his foot sank into a pothole and he tripped before he could reach her.

Bad luck.

"Undo what you did to Evelyn—and Anna," he demanded as he picked himself up off the ground.

Lady Luck smirked. "When it comes to Anna, she made a deal."

"And you're going to be okay with her getting hurt or possibly dying to pay for that deal?" He considered using his power on her, but the way he tripped showed that she was already using her power. There was no telling how his own magic might backfire.

"It's the terms that she agreed to. And it's how I get paid."

"Then how are you justifying what you're doing to Evelyn?"

"She's trying to stop me from making these deals. Just like you are." She reached for the slanted roof of the nearest garage and knocked on the framing three times.

Seconds later, the structure began to rattle. The next thing Frankie knew, the whole garage was tilting on its side and coming right toward him.

He jumped out of the way, inadvertently putting more space between him and Lady Luck.

Life before building standards meant a shoddy unsupported structure.

When Frankie had recovered from the fall, he saw Lady Luck running down the alley toward Holland Street. Jumping on the shingle tiles of the fallen roof, Frankie raced through the debris in pursuit of her.

She neared the end of the alley and he was afraid she

might make it to the street in time, so he extended his hand and waved it toward her feet.

To his surprise, it worked perfectly and she fell, smearing her white dress with even more dirt from the alley.

He slowed to a jog as he caught up to her. "What I don't understand is, why are you doing this? What are you really getting out of this?"

Lady Luck glared at him from behind her veil as she picked herself up again. "I collect souls. Sometimes, the bad luck only turns a good spirit into a disheartened one and I can't collect. More often, their bad luck leads to their death—whether accidentally or at their own hands. *That's* when I'm able to collect."

"So when it's just a disheartened spirit, that's when you plant thoughts in their heads and try to push them to end their lives themselves?"

She shrugged, the hint of a smirk evident on her lips. "Suicide."

Again, she shrugged. "What's the harm? With some, it doesn't take much convincing. And with Anna, I might not wait for her baby to be born to cash in on the deal. I see a double opportunity with her."

"No!" Frankie thrust both of his arms at her, putting all of his magical energy behind the attack.

But Lady Luck's good luck was on her side and his

magic backfired, sending *him* flying back from where he stood. He flipped over a fence and right into someone's backyard, where a dog was waiting on the other side.

At the sight of the intruder, the dog began snarling and barking at him. Frankie lifted himself off the grass and the dog took several nips at him, a warning to get out of his territory.

Annoyed, Frankie used his magic to push the dog away. It squealed as it flopped on its back and quickly regained its footing. Still, it kept a careful distance as Frankie climbed up the fence and launched himself over it.

Lady Luck waited on the other side with a wide, humorous smile. "What would've made that more perfect was if you landed in the dog's—"

"What is it going to take to get you to stop what you're doing?"

She smirked again. "I will never stop. Now, this is goodbye. I have deals to make." She started to leave, then turned back to him. "Oh, and don't try to stop me. You'll only embarrass yourself."

Frankie seethed with anger as he watched her walk off. What was he thinking, trying to come after her completely unprepared? He wasn't. He was reacting to what Lady Luck had done to Evelyn.

Lady Luck sauntered down toward the end of the

alley, likely feeling smug and untouchable.

Anna and Evelyn stepped into view at the end of the alley near Holland Street. Lady Luck stopped, took a quick look behind her, and started backing up.

From atop the chicken coop, Levi called down to Lady Luck. "Surprise!"

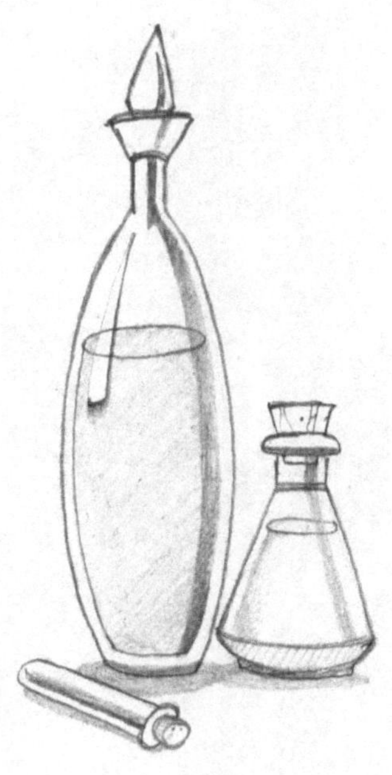

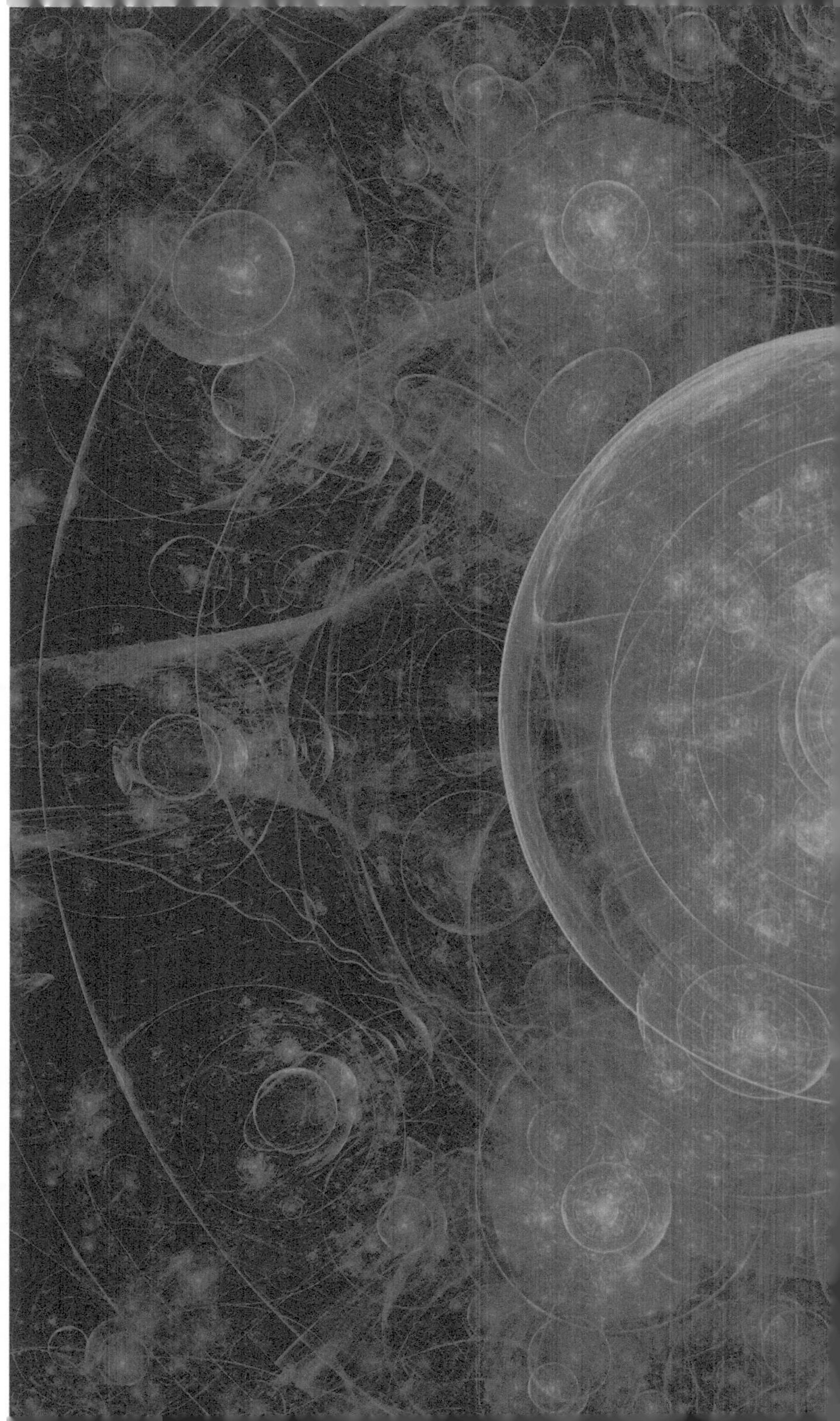

Chapter 32

- TUESDAY, MAY 19, 1970 -

The neighborhood grew more lively as the weather turned warmer. Even when the nights were still cool, people could be seen out walking their dogs later than usual or going for a jog. And then there were the cars that passed by, determined to get wherever they were going as quickly as possible, conveniently forgetting the danger their speed posed to themselves the people around them.

Frankie sat on the front steps of the house and watched the neighborhood move around him.

It had been on those front steps that his life had changed. The first glimpse he got of his wife's suicide. The first moment he realized his life would never be the same.

The mourners and well-wishers had finally cleared

out. Frankie's parents had agreed to move in right away, only spending the days at their house until they could get it packed up and sold. Suddenly the house was noisy again. But it was different.

Frankie needed to get away from that noise. He needed to clear his head. Think things through. Gary was right. The only way he was going to get through this was to spend some time in the raw emotions. As long as he was careful not to let those emotions whisk him away forever.

Samantha and Kathy needed him to stay strong.

The door opened behind him and Frankie turned to see his father coming out.

"Here." James handed him a jacket. "It's cold out here. Put this on before you get sick."

Frankie had barely noticed the temperature, but he complied simply to avoid any amount of bickering. As he moved, he noticed that he had been crying and wiped away the tears from his eyes.

"I also brought this out for you." James handed him a bottle of whiskey. "Today was rough. Nobody would blame you for taking the edge off for one night."

A genuine smiled spread across Frankie's face as he took the bottle and studied it. "Thanks, but I think I'm all set." He put it aside. Just like he couldn't let his emotions control him, he knew it would be too easy to drown his grief in alcohol. Better to keep it out of his life completely for a while.

"That's probably for the best," James said. "But I just thought I'd offer."

"I want to be fully-present for the girls," Frankie said. "How are they?"

"They're a little sadder now that it's night time. All they want is their mom."

Frankie nodded, feeling the tug at his heart. He had always been the one to put them to bed, but that was usually after the girls had spent all day with Marie. Now that she was gone, he needed to step up. So far, all he'd been doing was pushing off the extra responsibilities on his parents. On top of his grief, he also felt guilty of being a bad parent.

"I should go up and put them to bed." He started to rise, but James grabbed his arm and pulled him back down.

"Your mother has it under control. You can put them to bed tomorrow night. The three of you will need each other now more than ever. Your mother and I will be here to help, but we're still just Grandma and Grandpa."

"That's why it should be me up there."

James shook his head. "Not right now. Give yourself time to grieve your wife. Your girls will understand. They need to grieve too, but first they need to understand what had truly happened."

Frankie couldn't imagine answering all of their questions. He was so burned out from a long day of interaction and questions about the days leading up to his wife's passing that he needed time to recharge before he took on Samantha and Kathy's questions too.

"I just can't wrap my head around it," Frankie finally said. "The shock of it. Up until the last few days, Marie never seemed like the type who would…"

James nodded. "I know. I was thinking the same thing too."

Frankie scrutinized the last week of Marie's life. She had gone from taking the kids to the zoo and having a good time to blowing off a date with him and then —

"You know," James started quietly, "have you considered the possibility that she was led to end her own life supernaturally?"

As the potion soared through the air, Frankie expected to see Lady Luck's humor come to an abrupt end when she was splattered with the magical mixture. At the last second, however, a chicken jumped up and took the hit from the potion.

Lady Luck looked to the chicken, then looked to Frankie. "Once again, luck is on my side."

Frankie and Lady Luck's stare was broken as an egg came soaring through the air and smashed against her face. She opened her mouth in shock and turned to Levi, who stood at the chicken coop and launched egg after egg at her, although most landed around her.

"How dare you?" she declared.

Levi swung another one at her and she jumped out of the way.

With her distracted, Frankie jogged toward the end of the alley so he could check up on Anna.

"Are you okay?"

She nodded and stood up, although her face was still contorted in pain. "Yeah, I think it's just the baby kicking."

"Are you sure?" Frankie asked.

"No. I don't want the stress of all of this—or my bad luck—to have any harmful effects on the baby."

"Aw," Evelyn cooed. "We'll protect you." She squeezed Anna around the shoulders.

"Yeah," Frankie added. "Besides, if something were to happen to the baby, I would be the first to know. And I'm fine, so you have nothing to worry about."

Anna nodded and forced a smile. "So let's stop her so we can get out of here."

"I thought of something," Evelyn said.

Frankie cast a look back at Lady Luck and Levi. He still managed to fend her off with the eggs from the coop. But the eggs would likely run out sooner than later. He needed to get back to him.

"Can it wait?" Frankie asked.

"No—just hear me out," Evelyn said. "Lady Luck said she's also known as Fortuna or Tyche, right? Those are mythological names. In those myths, it's told that she was blindfolded so she could bestow her good and bad luck randomly, no matter the status, creed, or wellbeing of the receiver."

"Okay, well, she's clearly not blindfolded now. So am I supposed to convince her to put it back on? How's that going to stop her from taking it off?"

"I'm thinking maybe it was removed somehow and she liked being the one who decided who had luck and who didn't." Evelyn reached down and ripped off the bottom hem of her dress, which had already been torn. "Here. Try to blindfold her with this. Use your power."

Frankie nodded. "I'll give it a try."

Slowly, he wandered back to where Lady Luck and Levi were still dueling. He tried to stay behind her, so as not to tip her off. Levi, however, gave him away when he looked beyond her, directly at him.

Lady Luck turned. Frankie tossed the cloth in the air and then directed it toward Lady Luck's eyes with his magic. She swatted it out of the air and it fell to the ground.

Frankie dove to the ground to retrieve it, but before he could get there, one of the chickens rushed over and began tearing the fabric to shreds.

As Lady Luck approached the spot where the fabric had fallen, she smiled. "Don't you see it by now? You'll never be able to stop me. I'm the goddess of chance."

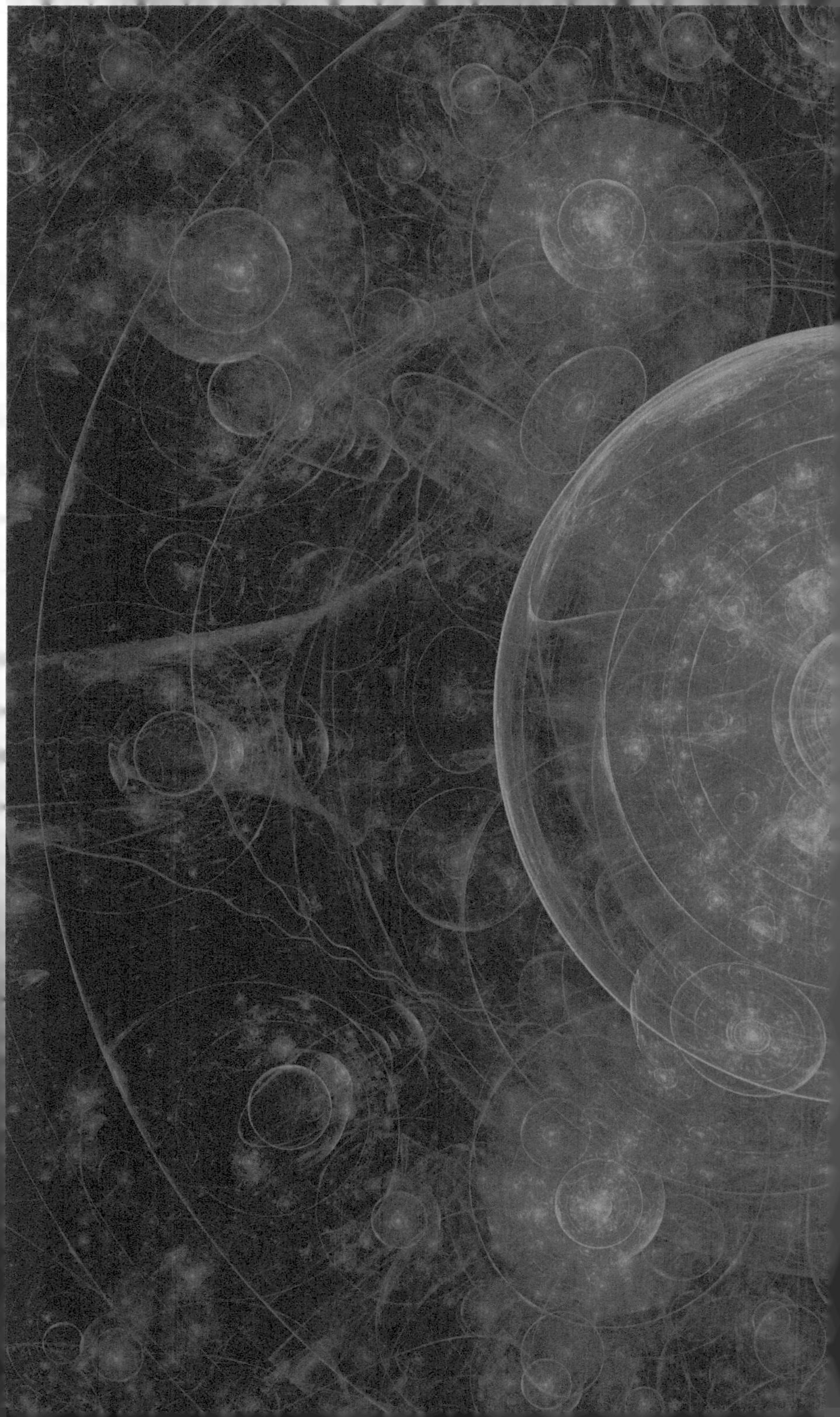

CHAPTER 34

- TUESDAY, MAY 19, 1970 -

Frankie sat on the couch in the living room after everyone had gone to bed. He still couldn't bring himself to spend a night in his own bed. The same one he had shared with his wife. The last place he saw her alive. It would take a long time before he was able to bring himself to do that.

For now, he sat in the dim light of a single lamp as the clock crept closer to midnight. He flipped through the wrinkled pages of *The Art of Magic*, searching for the witch that Marie had encountered the week before at the zoo.

After what his father had suggested, it seemed like the only logical explanation for Marie's sudden turn to suicide. More than that, it was the last shred of hope that he had to hold on to. That his wife had been pushed supernaturally to her death, and that he could get justice for her passing.

The problem was, he couldn't remember the name of the woman Marie had found in the book. But he had a faint recollection of the illustration that accompanied the entry. All he needed to do was lay eyes on it and he would recognize her. It would take time, but he was willing to go through each page if he had to. He was a man on a mission.

Halfway through the book, he had still come up empty. For a brief moment, he considered waking his parents up and asking them, but immediately pushed the thought aside. Marie had said that she didn't even mention the encounter with the evil witch to them because she thought it was so insignificant.

Clearly, if his father's suggestion was correct, Marie's thought had been wrong.

Finally, Frankie turned to a page that he instantly recognized. The name at the top read "Morta." The entry didn't specify what kind of threat she was. Apparently, whomever had first encountered her in the Walker family didn't get a lot of details about her threat level. Which meant that Frankie was back at square one. He didn't know if Morta was truly the reason his wife was dead.

He sat back against the couch, feeling relief in his aching back, while simultaneously being consumed with dread. How could he get justice for her death if he didn't know a thing about the last supernatural threat she had faced? What if this Morta decided to come after another part of his family? If someone else he loved died, he wouldn't be able to live with himself.

An idea struck him. Setting the book aside, Frankie got up to retrieve several items for a spell. He went to a cabinet in the foyer and gathered three candles of varying colors: silver, pink, and brown. Then he went upstairs into the bathroom and grabbed Marie's hairbrush that still sat beside the sink where she had left it the last time she had used it.

Back in the living room, he set the three candles in the shape of a triangle and stood in the center. After lighting each one, he pulled free several strands of hair that had clung to the bristles of Marie's hairbrush. Slowly, he dipped his wife's hair into the flame of one of the candles and recited the spell:

Marie, can you hear my cry?
Across the oceans and the skies?
From the place where you have gone,
follow the light to guide you home.

Lucky by Magic

Magical wind began to stir around the room, but soon died off. What followed was nothing but silence.

"Damn it," Frankie groaned. He considered trying the spell again, but decided against it. If that one hadn't worked, he would try a different one. There was still some of Marie's hair on the brush.

He blew out the silver and brown candles and returned them to the cabinet, where he retrieved blue and white ones instead. Again, he laid them out in a triangle pattern with the already-lit pink candle. The different colors of the candles would ignite different feelings with the spell that would—hopefully—power it enough for the desired outcome.

This time, he went to the kitchen and gathered various herbs that were listed in the book, under the spell, "To Summon a Loved One."

With the white willow bark, gum arabic, poke root, and hibiscus chopped up and mixed together in a copper ritual bowl, Frankie dipped his wife's hair in the flame of one of the candles and dropped it into the bowl as he recited:

Blood of my blood, answer my plea.
Through time and space, wherever you may be.

He tried this spell again with more vigor and power

to his voice. While the wind stirred like the last spell, it quickly died out. Once again, Frankie was surrounded by the dark loneliness.

Swinging his fist, Frankie punched the couch cushion in anger. As he blew out the candles and began to clean up his ritual work, he could hear the floorboards shifting upstairs.

Someone was awake.

He only hoped that it wasn't Samantha or Kathy. They deserved a good night's rest. Grief was an exhausting rollercoaster ride and the girls were simply too young to handle all of the emotions flowing through their tiny bodies.

But as Frankie returned the candles to the cabinet in the foyer, he saw his father coming down in his bathrobe.

"Are you okay? I heard banging." He glanced at the candles Frankie was putting away. "And chanting."

"I'm fine, Dad. Go back to sleep."

James indicated the cabinet. "You were performing a ritual."

"So?"

"You need to be careful."

"About what?" Frankie asked. "I know what I'm doing."

LUCKY BY MAGIC

James raised his eyebrows. "And you're determined to do it alone?"

Frankie was quiet for a while. Finally, he murmured, "I have to."

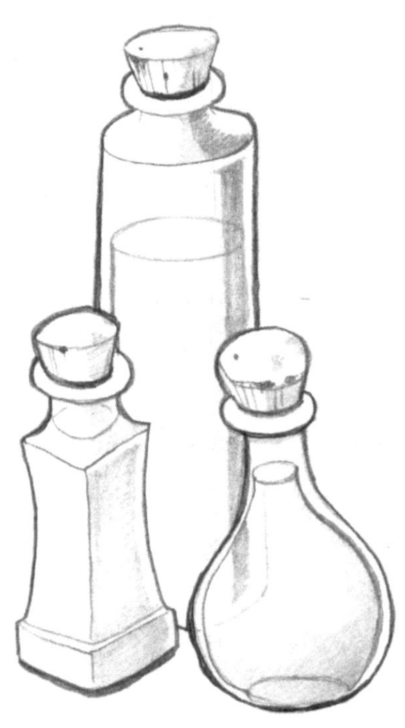

CHAPTER 35

Frankie looked back toward Evelyn. "Any other ideas?"

Lady Luck laughed again and stepped toward Frankie, who took a careful step backward. Then she turned toward Levi, who took his own step in the opposite direction. His foot crunched against the eggshell from his failed attempt to subdue Lady Luck.

"You see, as the goddess of chance, anything is within my power," she said. "I don't even need to dream it up. I simply need to apply the right amount of luck and then the universe takes it from there."

Levi looked down at the bits of eggshell stuck to the bottom of his foot, and then his eyes snapped up to

Frankie. "The eggs!"

Everyone turned to him. Initially, Frankie was just as confused as everyone else. Then he saw the shattered shells stuck to Levi's foot and he understood.

He looked around and saw that the shattered eggshells were all over the alley around them.

"Hey lady!" Frankie called to her. "Watch this!" He waved up his hands and each piece of the broken shells rose up in the air with the assistance of his power. With another flick of his hands in her direction, the shells formed two steady streams that pelted Lady Luck's eyeballs like gunfire.

The attack hit Lady Luck with a force that rocked her head backward. Immediately, she clawed at her eyes and let out a shriek of pain. She fell to her knees and tried to paw away the shells from her eyes, but the blood draining down her face made it evident that the damage had been done.

"Ugh," Evelyn groaned from behind Frankie.

Anna gasped for air and he spun around to look at her.

"Are you okay?" he asked.

"No!" Lady Luck cried out. "I can't see!"

Frankie ignored her and ran to his pregnant grandmother. "How's my father doing?"

She rubbed her belly and nodded, a smile creeping

across her face. "Much better. I feel like a weight has been lifted from my shoulders."

"Lady Luck's magic must've worn off when she lost her sight," Evelyn said.

"And how are you doing?" Frankie asked.

"Much better. They gave me a dose of the potion before we left the house, which reversed the effects of her magic. Now, hopefully everyone who made a deal with her will be safe."

"The balance of the world has been restored," Anna said. "Luck is blind once again."

"Hey!" Levi called as he ran up to them. "I know she's been misbehaving and all, but we need to get Lady Luck some help. The way she's screaming, people are starting to look."

Frankie nodded. "Her eyesight is definitely gone. There's nothing that will be able to bring it back. Why don't you tell someone to call an ambulance?"

Levi nodded and then ran up to the house with the chicken coop. There was a man standing on the back porch, who Levi toward.

"What are we going to do with Lady Luck?" Evelyn asked.

Frankie looked over his shoulder in her direction. "Leave her. The first responders will come and take care of her. Nobody is going to believe anything she says.

They're going to be more concerned with her eyes than anything."

"That was personal for you," Anna said. "What she was doing to her victims. Wasn't it?"

Frankie was quiet for a moment, then looked to the ground and nodded. "Nobody has the right to mess with someone's head like that. Life is bad enough already. We don't need to be pushing people down even more."

Anna rubbed his shoulder. "Thanks to you, Lady Luck won't be able to do that anymore."

Frankie felt previous regrets sneak up on him and he looked away from Anna. He cleared his throat. "We should probably get out of here before the police show up and start asking questions."

"Yeah," Evelyn said softly. "I'll go get Levi."

After she left, Frankie and Anna stood quietly. Frankie didn't want to say anymore—he didn't even want to *think* about it anymore. Picking up on that, Anna simply reached out for his hand and squeezed it tight. A quiet reminder that he wasn't alone.

CHAPTER 36

While the seance spells that Frankie had tried the night before had been complete and utter failures, there was a spell that *had* worked: the tried and true location ritual. With it, Frankie had tracked down Morta to St. Vincent Hospital on W 25th Street.

As he arrived, he saw Morta lingering just around the corner from the main entry, near two service doors. Clearly, she was looking for her next victim.

Frankie parked the car and made eye contact with the witch as he got out of the car.

Morta's eyes widened when she saw him and she darted across the street toward the parking garage.

Frankie took after her at a run.

"Hey!" he barked.

There was an elderly couple walking along the row of cars toward the hospital entry who looked at him as he shouted, but they continued walking toward the hospital.

At the moment, Frankie didn't care about exposing him magic. All he wanted was to get revenge for his wife's death.

The evil witch was quick as she ran, her stringy, straw-like hair bouncing off her shoulders as she moved in a fast, but drunken way. And yet she was surprisingly fast. She made it to the first ramp and started rounding the corner.

Frankie feared he was going to lose her and so he held up his hand to send the witch rolling across the pavement. The magical assist gave him enough time to catch up to her.

Grabbing her by the front of her robe, Frankie slammed her against a concrete pillar and leaned in close to her wrinkled, mottled face.

"You're the reason my wife is dead!"

Morta cackled. "I thought she committed suicide?"

Rage flared through Frankie's body at her laughter and he swung a fist right at her face. Immediately, the witch's nose began to bleed, although she still laughed with blood-smeared teeth.

"That little witch thought she could stop me, but she had her own demons to worry about," Morta said through cackles. "Didn't she?"

"The only demons my wife had were the kind who preyed on children—and the vulnerable." He swung another punch at her, feeling something break in her mouth.

Morta spit out pieces of her teeth into Frankie's face. "Punch me all you want. Your wife will still be dead. And there isn't a damn thing you can do about it!"

"I'm going to kill you for this!" he muttered.

Again, the witch gave him a broken smile. "There's nothing you can do to me that would take away the high I got from leading the witch into insanity. And now her soul is burning in hell for taking her own life!"

All sense of self-control left Frankie. Using his magic for added power, he began to swing his fist at Morta's face repeatedly, pummeling her again and again with the added force of his power. After a minute, the cackle faded and her body went limp. As the dead witch slunk to the oil-stained pavement, the broken smile was still evident on her face.

Frankie was so consumed by his rage that he didn't hear the truck pull up behind him. It wasn't until James grabbed his arms and pulled him away from Morta that

Lucky by Magic

Frankie realized what he had done.

The sight of the battered witch—and the blood on his own hands—caused Frankie to hyperventilate. What had he done? This wasn't justice. This was murder. Magic only assisted in this execution. The rest had been done with his own bare hands.

"Easy, easy," James muttered to his son. "Take a deep breath. Relax. Come on."

Frankie sank into his father's arms as another wave of emotions came over him: grief. Unhindered, natural grief. The kind that felt like it would physically rip Frankie to shreds.

James wrapped his son in a bear-hug from behind and the two of them sat still for a moment while Frankie cried.

"You know," James started slowly, "we need to get the body out of here."

Frankie stood up straighter and nodded his head, sucking in a shuddering breath.

James, meanwhile, looked around for onlookers or security cameras. Neither were in sight. "It's early yet, so the hospital is not that busy, but it's going to be soon. We don't have much time."

"What do we do?"

"Help me get the body in the truck."

"But where—"

James held up his hand. "Don't ask questions until we're alone."

Between the two of them, they lifted Morta's bloodied and broken body into the bed of the truck. James covered the body in a tarp and made sure it was secured strapped down, so it didn't blow away in the wind. James held the door open for his son to climb into the passenger seat, then James got behind the steering wheel and drove off.

CHAPTER 37

The altar contained red candles for love and strength, as well as white candles for peace, light, and unity. Periwinkle was sprinkled around the table, along with amulets and talismans that Anna had pulled together to strengthen the spell. As part of the ritual setup, she also burned incense around her living room, where she sat with Frankie and Evelyn to cast the spell.

Levi had stayed behind to work the restaurant. After skipping out on the dinner rush the night before, he thought it was fair that he picked up the breakfast and lunch shifts to make up for it.

Frankie stood in front of the altar while Evelyn and Anna surrounded him with their interlocked hands. The

Lucky by Magic

women chanted the spell three times.

It was a spell that Anna had crafted overnight in preparation for this moment. When Frankie and Evelyn arrived that morning, Anna already had everything set up and ready to go. Anna thought that her power, combined with her baby's power, along with Evelyn's power, and boosted by the amulets and talismans she had, would be enough to send Frankie back to his rightful time.

However, as they chanted the spell, the wind stirred and faint chimes could be heard, but after they finished chanting the third time, all of the magical rumblings they had stirred up dissipated completely.

"It didn't work," Frankie said.

"Try reciting it with us this time," Anna said. "Three times. Stay where you are. You're the center of the incantation. Again. With *feeling* this time!"

We call to the keepers of time and space.
Return this man to his family's embrace.

This time, the wind stirred even more, shaking the curtains against the windows and the houseplants in the corner. Once again, when they finished chanting, nothing happened.

After the second time, Anna was the only one who wasn't discouraged.

Frankie groaned and flopped back onto the couch. "I'm beginning to think that I'm going to permanently be stuck in 1924."

Anna, who had returned to *The Art of Magic* to look for additional boosters, held up a finger. "We don't know for sure that that's the case. We may only need another witch or another amulet or another herb to power this spell even further."

Evelyn shook her head. "The trouble is, I can't see any future where Frankie returns to 1984."

Frankie buried his head in his hands.

"That doesn't mean it's impossible," Anna was quick to add. "Evelyn, before Frankie first arrived, did you foresee his arrival in our time?"

"Well…no, but now that he's here, I *do* see him in this time."

"That's because he's already here." Anna looked to

Frankie. "It's not impossible, only more difficult. With magic, we can accomplish anything. Don't give up hope."

"Well, short of Zanabar showing up and taking me back to my time with no strings attached, then I think I am stuck." He got up and walked to the front window, looking out onto the street that looked completely different from the one that he remembered.

"Oh! We could ask William to help with the spell," Anna suggested. "He's a witch too."

"Honestly, it's probably best if fewer people—especially people from my own family—know about me and where I'm actually from," Frankie said. He didn't mention the fact that he remembered his grandfather very well, into his adulthood. If William remembered Frankie from 1924, what kind of effect would that have on the future?

Anna nodded. "I understand. I just want to make sure that you get home to your family. To your daughters."

"Me too. But in the meantime I'm stuck here and I feel completely powerless. All I want to do is get home to them without screwing up the future that I remember."

"By not making any connections to anyone?" Anna asked.

Frankie glanced over at Evelyn, then back to Anna. "I've made connections."

"Besides Evelyn and Levi, who do you talk to?"

"Um..."

"What job do you have?"

"Levi's restaurant."

"Where are you living?"

"Above Levi's restaurant..."

Anna raised her eyebrows. "Just what I thought. You've completely isolated yourself. That's no way to go through life, keeping your distance from everyone."

Frankie nodded. "I know, but spending a life away from my girls is a terrible existence anyway. You'll understand that really soon when my father is born."

The young witch pursed her lips and averted her eyes, while she rested her hands on her belly. "Yes, well. I suppose my parental instincts might not have kicked in yet. However, I know a thing or two about wanting to fit in. Everyone has felt that way at some point."

"My concern," Evelyn said quietly, "is that Frankie isn't a part of this time. His mere presence here has changed things. I think there is some credibility to his worries that he's going to alter his own future the longer he stays in our time."

"I need to get back home," Frankie added. "Sooner than later."

Lucky by Magic

The room was quiet as they all struggled to find the impossible solution. Frankie knew that the root of the problem, no matter how well-intentioned everyone had been, was that the witches in 1924 simply didn't have enough power to get him back to 1984. Time travel required a high level of magic. And since each generation of magic was stronger than the previous, he was unlikely to find someone with enough power to help him sixty years before his own time. Especially when he didn't know of any magical being—other than Zanabar—who could successfully complete time travel. Even in 1984, witches didn't have that power.

"For what it's worth," Anna spoke up, "at least you *do* have some friends here. And you have me too. It may be wise for us to keep our distance from each other, but I'll still be here if you ever need help again."

Frankie smiled. "Thanks. I appreciate that."

"I may not have met my own child yet, but somehow—through the mystery of magic—I've met my grandchild first. Even though we only met yesterday, just know that I love you."

CHAPTER 38

Watching Marie's murderer burn in a pyre gave a certain sense of closure to her sudden passing. However, as Frankie watched the flames engulf Morta, he was still full of rage. Full of grief. Full of shock and denial. It would take a long time to get over his wife's death. She had been the center of his world. Of their daughters' worlds. And now she was gone.

James stood beside his son, quietly watching the pyre burn as well. He had driven about twenty-five minutes outside of the city to a quiet road not far from Waterford. They had found a walking path that led to a swamp. It had been dry enough that James was able to pull his truck right back and toss Morta's body into the pyre.

With a magical assist to ensure that the flames would be hot enough to erase any trace of Morta's body, they set it on fire so that the evil witch had no chance of returning and tormenting anyone else again.

"Marie didn't deserve to die," Frankie murmured.

"No, she didn't."

"She was manipulated by Morta. Tortured."

"And now we've taken care of the woman who did that to her."

Frankie shook his head and thought about the last two days he had spent with Marie. How much she must've suffered quietly. "I missed all of the signs."

"You didn't know what she was thinking," James said. "You couldn't have known."

"I should've asked her more about Morta when Marie first saw her."

"She kept it a secret. None of us knew exactly what happened. Depending on what magic had been placed on her, maybe Marie didn't even know."

Frankie was quiet as he watched the flames and heard the fire crackle and pop. The black smoke wafted into the air, but in the rural setting nobody would much notice the smoke billowing in the air.

"There was something Morta said," Frankie said

quietly. "Right before I…"

"Don't put too much stock in what she said to you," James warned. "She was probably trying to manipulate you like she manipulated Marie."

Frankie shook his head. "No, she said that Marie's soul is burning in hell because she committed suicide. What if that's true? What if Marie's still suffering?"

James shook his head and turned to his son. "No. You can't think like that. Marie's gone. She was a good person. Her soul is at peace. You cannot believe the words her murderer said right before—"

"Right before I killed her?" Frankie's question hung in the air. He didn't regret what he had done. Not really. But it did pose the question: how was one death a tragedy and another death justice?

"No matter what happened," James went on, "you need to focus on mourning the loss of your wife and picking up the pieces. For yourself. For your girls. For everyone in your life who loves you." He put his arm around his son's shoulders and stared back into the pyre. "I know it's hard, but you have to find a way to move forward."

It would be impossible for Frankie to move forward. He couldn't imagine a world without Marie in it. Sure, his parents would be there to help with Samantha and Kathy, but his parents weren't a true replacement for their mother. Their relationship with their mother was robbed from them by Morta.

There was one thing he was certain of, though. Despite how Marie died, it was not suicide. She had been murdered. If it wasn't for Aorta's magic, Marie would still be alive today. And now, burning in the magical flame before him, his wife's murderer was dead herself.

PICK UP THE FINAL BOOK IN THE SERIES, **LURED BY MAGIC**, AND LET THE FIGHT CONTINUE!

DAVIDNETHBOOKS.COM/LOSTBYMAGIC

SUICIDE HOTLINE

If you or a loved one is considering suicide, please utilize the following resources:

Call/Text: 988 (in the U.S.)

Visit online: https://988lifeline.org/

BEHIND THE BOOK:
LUCKY BY MAGIC

One of the things I love about the way I wrote these Lost by Magic books is that I got to fill in the gaps of some story details that had been missing throughout the Art of Magic series. Details that are too small to dedicate a whole book to, but are too important to hide away in a short story that most readers will miss.

With *Lucky by Magic*, I wanted to dive into what happened to Frankie's wife, Marie, but still leave things open to dive into Marie's story more in the future (which is already in the works in *Necromancer*, Coven Book 11). The story leading up to Marie's death is a very sad one, but also a very important one. As a wife and a mother, she has immense influence on so many people in her lives, and her sudden, abrupt, and tragic departure leaves them all handling the loss in different ways. We see how her daughters handle her loss in the Coven series, and we see glimpses of how Frankie handle her loss throughout the Lost by Magic series.

Beyond Marie's story, I really liked the idea of Lady Luck as a character. Someone who is a bit mysterious and powerful, but in a very different sense. She's not a big-magic, showy kind of power. Hers is more subtle, relying on her influence over other's people's actions.

I liked toying with the power that luck plays in people's lives, and how it manifests itself in different ways. Good luck and bad luck is not an end-all, be-all. It's an influence, sure, and a presence that plays a part in your position, but cannot overcome hard work and dedication.

One of the newer characters in this book that felt so natural to write was Anna, Frankie's grandmother. When I first started this series, I knew that I wanted Frankie to meet part of his family, but I also knew that he would need to tread carefully so that he didn't mess up the timeline in the future. Still, it was fun to tell more of the history of the Walker family, including some of the history of the Walker house and how that has evolved over time, and the people who played a part in making it what it is throughout the Art of Magic universe.

This book was primarily written in August 2022. Even though I tried to maintain the same schedule and pace as I had when I wrote *Lost by Magic* in July 2022 (write in the mornings, work on publishing administrative stuff, get son from daycare, go for a walk, put him down for a nap, read until he woke up), I struggled while writing this book.

August turns out to be busy in a very different way than July. My birthday is August 4th, so I try not to work on my birthday. My family likes to go on a big family vacation every year and in 2022, that vacation took place in August. And while I enjoy those vacations and taking time off, it is still time away from writing that needs to be accounted for. Also, being that I'm a school librarian, I felt more pressure on myself to get this book done before I returned to work at the end of August. Add to that a more independent toddler whose nap schedule changes daily…

So yeah, this book was more challenging to write, logistically speaking. But I did it! And I'm very happy with this book!

Like with *Lost by Magic*, by time it came to editing this book, I took full advantage of my free periods at work to keep everything moving forward, even as the fall led into the holidays and I had to juggle work, the holidays, and other writing commitments.

I hope you enjoyed this book, and are enjoying the series! Please leave a review online to let everyone know what you thought of the book. Even a simple star rating, or a one-sentence review goes a long way in helping spread the word about my books and helps me apply for promotions. And, as always, feel free to email me to let me know what you thought of the book! I love hearing from readers!

Thanks for reading!

Acknowledgments

This project would not have been possible without the support of my Kickstarter backers! Thank you all for your support!

Julian White - Pauline Baird Jones - Leslie Twitchell - John Idlor - Dead Fishie - Rhys Everly-Lawless - Debbie Phillips - Samantha Ghormley - Andrew French - Ian the Badlyironed - Karen Tankersley - Claudia Klein - Becky Carr - René Fuentes - Amber Beck - Anthea Sharp - Rowan Stone - Rachelle Degoumois - Ashley Britt - RJ Hopkinson - Hope Terrell - Chad Bowden - Daniel Dickerson - Bill Garrett - Erik S - Gary Phillips - Felicitas Odemer - Philip J. Carpenter - A

How much is your soul worth?

After thinking that they're hunting a crossroads demon, Frankie and his friends discover that Hecate is in town, and she's after innocent souls. The gatekeeper of the underworld sends phantoms, who takes the shape of someone from the victim's past, and torments them until they decide to trade in their soul to end the suffering.

While trying to find a way to stop the goddess, Evelyn finds herself trapped in an alternate plane, where she witnesses Hecate quietly wreaking havoc of those around her. And the longer she spends in the alternate plane, the weaker she becomes.

Meanwhile, Frankie is suddenly seeing his late wife, who tries to persuade him to join her in the afterlife so they can spend eternity together.

As Hecate closes in on the group, Levi is the only one who can see what's going on. And as the only one without magic of his own, saving his friends might be an impossible task.

Lured by Magic is the third book in the Lost by Magic series, which serves as the first series in the Art of Magic universe, containing the Coven and the Under the Moon series.

LURED BY MAGIC

LOST BY MAGIC: BOOK 3

Read on for an excerpt of the final book in
the Lost by Magic series!

DAVID NETH

CHAPTER 1

Tommy Rindell finished mopping up the floor in the dining room of Meyer's Place after closing. He was grateful that Levi had hired him at the restaurant, but it wasn't Tommy's favorite job he'd ever had. Still, the money was okay, especially when Levi pulled him from the kitchen when one of the waitresses called in sick.

Not that that happened often.

Rolling the mop bucket back into the cleaning closet, Tommy did a once-over in the kitchen to make sure everything was cleaned and ready for the breakfast rush in the morning.

"Go on and get out of here," Levi said from behind

him. He was counting bills at the bar, but glanced up and smiled at Tommy. "You've had a long enough day as it is."

Tommy flashed a smile. "You sure?"

"Positive. Have a good night. See you tomorrow." Levi turned his attention back to the cash.

Tommy grabbed his coat from the rack and set out toward the trolley line.

It was late, but he was usually able to catch the final ride out. Sometimes, if Levi needed extra help after closing, Tommy had to walk all the way home. Even with a quick pace, it still took him about an hour.

Luckily, today was not one of those days.

As Tommy got on the trolley and paid the fare, he counted the rest of the cash in his wallet. There wasn't much, and payday didn't come until the end of the week. Even if Levi let him out on time the rest of the week, there was no way Tommy would be able to afford to take the trolley every night. Not if he wanted to eat too.

Ever since his father had passed away from the influenza epidemic the year before, the weight of the household finances fell on Tommy's shoulders. And he didn't have much. A modest house on the outskirts of town. His mother had run out on them right before his father became ill, so now it was just Tommy left to take care of everything.

And there wasn't any inheritance to speak of. His father could barely rub two pennies together himself. It was one of the reasons Tommy needed to quit school and start working. They needed the money. But after his father went and died on him, Tommy was back to a single-income household. Even though he was a family of one, it still cost a certain amount to maintain his modest lifestyle. An amount that Tommy could barely keep a handle on.

The trolley dropped him off at the corner of W 26th and Raspberry Streets. His house was only a short walk from there.

After the trolley pulled away, the darkness of the night truly set in. The city had yet to install streetlights in his developing neighborhood, leaving the few dim houselights the only illumination to guide him. Even the moon was hidden behind the clouds.

At the crossroads of W 27th and Raspberry, Tommy stared in the direction of the intersection. There was a shadow there, but he couldn't make out quite what it was. He began to turn to head to his house, but terrifying thoughts filled his mind.

What if it's an animal that wants to jump me?

What if it's a murderer who wants to kill me?

What if it's someone in trouble who could use my help?

Lured by Magic

"He-Hello?" he called out nervously. "Is somebody there?"

The shadow moved again, only this time Tommy's eyes were blinded as a torch lit up in flames in her hand.

She wore a dark robe and had a set of skeleton keys hanging from the arm opposite the torch. And she was beautiful, with dark hair framing her porcelain face and eyes that seemed to see right through to his soul.

"Who are you?" he asked. "And why are you standing in the middle of the road? You're going to get hit."

"Do you need help?" she asked.

Tommy's brow furrowed. "Me? I was just walking home. Are you stuck? What's going on?"

She smirked. "No, I'm not stuck."

"Then why are you in the middle of the street?"

"It's the in-between," she explained. "I assure you, it's not as dangerous as it seems."

Tommy studied her, not sure what to make of her. He considered ignoring her and walking off to his house. But that was rude. He may have been poor, but he was always polite. And what if she wished him harm? Did he really want to lead her right to his meager home? But she was just a woman. Surely, she wasn't capable of hurting anyone.

"Come here." The skeleton keys on her wrist jangled

as she raised her arm out toward him, her hand extended in his direction.

Tommy considered her command. He could just go home and pretend that none of this had happened. She would be gone in the morning. He could forget about it then.

But a bigger part of him wanted to go to her. Wanted to talk to her. Maybe more. He craved true human connection. And maybe a stranger in the street was just the person to help him with that.

Hesitantly, he stepped out into the intersection toward the woman. His eyes darted left, then right, looking out for any vehicles that might come racing by in the darkness. None came. The night was eerily still. Like they were frozen in time.

When he was in front of her, she reached up and stroked his cheek. She tutted her tongue three times. "Aw, I know you've been having a hard time lately. So lonely. Struggling to keep your head above water. No one to lean on."

"How do you—do I know you?"

"I knew your father."

His eyes grew wide. "You did? How? From where?" A young, attractive woman would've certainly come up at some point if his father had crossed paths with her.

"He was down on his luck not that long ago, either,"

she went on. "A dark place. I helped him out."

"Helped him out how? He never mentioned you."

She smiled. "As he promised he would. Your father and I made a deal. He was desperate and agreed to my terms."

"What terms?"

"I helped him have an easier life in return for payment after he died."

"You mean, like—"

"His soul," she cut in.

"You took his soul?"

She smirked. "It was the term he agreed to. Haven't you ever wondered how he always managed to have food on the table, even when he was between jobs? Or how he would always get a job offer, right after he quit one?"

"That was *you*?" Tommy couldn't believe it. Was this a dream? He was tired enough to believe that it might be. Maybe he would wake up in the morning with no recollection that any of this happened. Maybe he was imagining it, desperate to have some sort of respite to his tiring life.

"I'm capable of anything, for the right price," she went on. "Your father was desperate and I helped him. Now, the question is: are you desperate enough to agree to the same terms?"

CHAPTER 2

"So what exactly are we looking for?" Levi asked Evelyn as they came up to the intersection of W 27th Street and Raspberry Street. Night had fallen and the chilly fall breeze blew the crunchy leaves across the dirt road.

She squinted in the darkness. "I'm not exactly sure. My vision was murky."

"So then why are we here?" Frankie asked from her other side.

"All of my divination readings said that something bad happened at this corner."

"Which one?" Levi pointed. "There are four corners here. Were they on the sidewalk?"

She shook her head. "No. In the street."

"How can you tell?" Frankie asked. "It's so dark. Would it kill them to put in some streetlights?"

"This far out from town?" Levi commented. "Why would they?"

Frankie laughed. "Where I come from, this is damn well near the center of town."

"Don't even start with the whole 'I'm from the future' bit," Levi said with a groan.

"Would you both be quiet?" she snapped. "We're not going to be able to hear anything if you keep talking."

"Evelyn, look around!" Frankie gestured toward the intersection. "There's nothing here. And unless you have something concrete from your vision to go on, then I think we're just wasting our time."

The oracle wasn't convinced. "I just have a feeling…"

Frankie sighed and decided to give her break. He knew very well that nagging magical intuition feeling. He stepped out into the intersection and looked around, trying to find any remnants of the supernatural thread that Evelyn had picked up on.

The biggest thing that he noticed was that the area felt familiar to him. The newly-built house on the corner was his first sale as a realtor in 1984. How strange it was to see it at its infancy.

But there was something else. Underneath the familiarity. Something big that was hiding. Subdued. As if someone else didn't want the enormity of it to be found out.

"What is it?" Levi asked from beside Frankie. He hadn't seen him approach in the darkness.

The witch nodded. "I agree with Evelyn. There's a supernatural presence here. A dark one, at that."

"I told you," Evelyn said.

Levi looked between the two of them. "How do you know?"

"I can feel it," Frankie said. "The same thing Evelyn's picking up on."

Levi raised his eyebrows. "I don't feel anything."

"That's because you're nonmagical," Frankie explained. "You don't have the magical intuition the rest of us do. The one that picks up when something is just a bit off. Which is exactly how certain evils operate. They take advantage of the nonmagical who can't sense magical dangers themselves."

"It's like a sixth-sense," Evelyn added. "If the power is great enough, sometimes we can sense the magical workings happening around us. Or, in this case, what had previous transpired."

"And if they're really skilled—or if we're not seeking it out—even we can miss it ourselves." Frankie looked over at Evelyn. "That's why I didn't immediately pick up on it, either."

"Okay, so then what exactly are you guys *feeling*?" Levi asked.

Both Frankie and Evelyn said nothing, but looked around the dark, quiet, chilly neighborhood.

Finally, Frankie turned to Evelyn. "Do you think you can get a vision to recall anything that happened here?"

"I can try, but from what I can tell, there's something blocking my power." Still, she crouched to the ground and held her hands out to the dirt road, where the two streets intersected. She closed her eyes and concentrated, sitting quietly for a long time. Then, after several moments of fierce determination, she rose to her feet and shook her head.

"Nothing?" Frankie asked.

"I just feel a bad presence," she explained. "I couldn't call up a vision."

"So does that mean that everything's fine?" Levi asked.

Frankie and Evelyn exchanged more looks between them.

"That's...not necessarily the case," Frankie said.

"Sometimes there's a magic stronger than mine that is able to block my psychic interferences," Evelyn said.

"Someone is actively trying to hide whatever happened here."

"But you got the first vision unprompted," Levi said. "Back at the restaurant."

"That must've been before the protections were placed."

The trio fell silent as they looked around the darkness.

"So what do we do next?" Levi asked.

"We need to start digging," Frankie said.

"For clues?"

He shook his head. "Yes. In the ground."

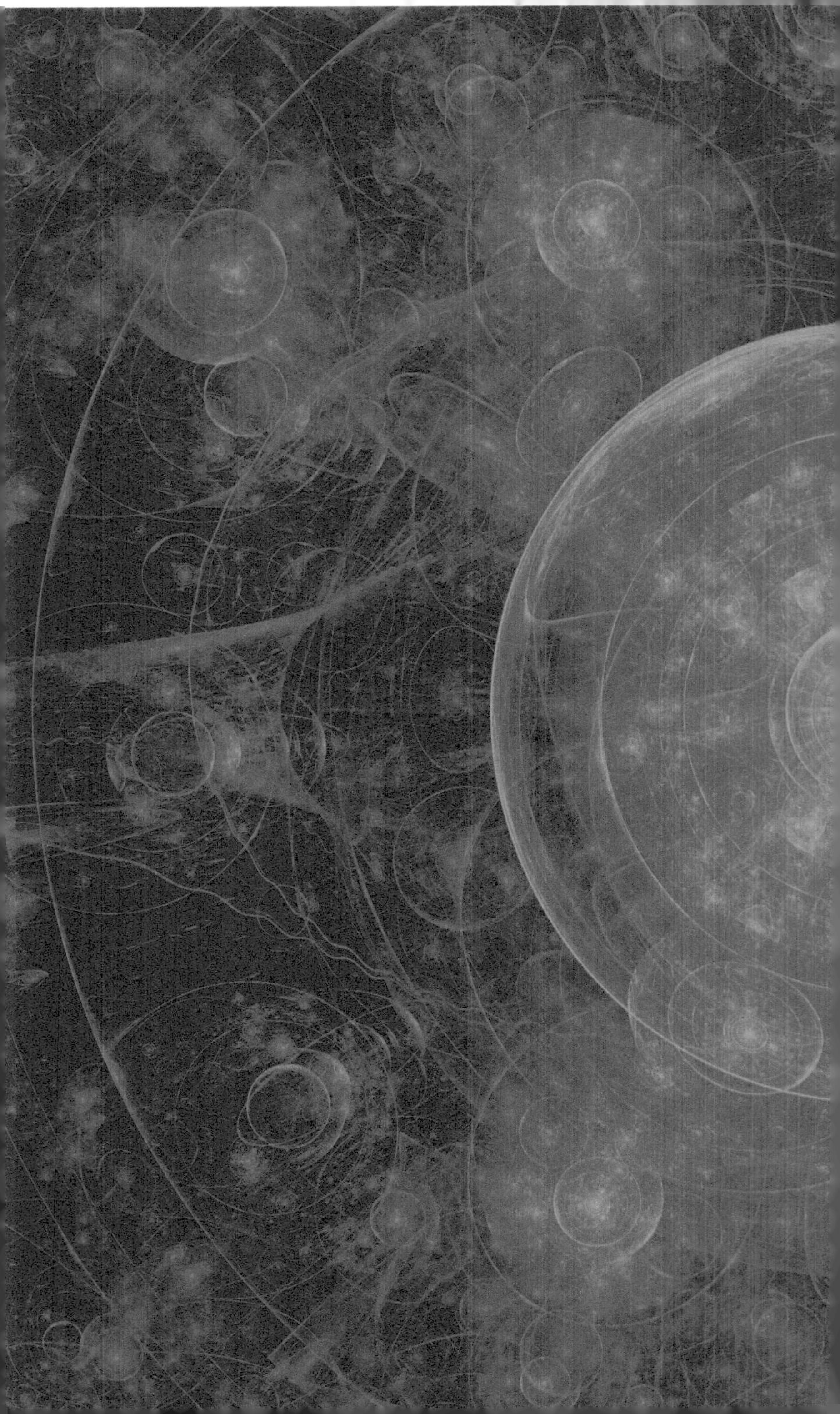

CHAPTER 3

Eddie McDonald parked on W 27th Street and walked to the front porch of his house, which was on the corner with Raspberry Street. He was exhausted, having worked ten hours at the rail yards doing mostly manual labor. The idea of a cold beer sounded like heaven.

Although, truth be told, he had been trying to have as little alcohol as possible. It didn't help his mental state any and, after his wife had left him, he hadn't been doing so hot.

Home was no comfort. He and his wife had bought the house as a starter house in their third year of marriage. Eddie had been anxious to get out of the cramped apartment that they lived in downtown. Judy, on the other hand, seemed a little disinterested in the idea of buying a house.

That should've been his first clue that something was wrong in their marriage. Of course, in the moment it was hard to tell.

Now, a year after they had bought the house together, he was a single homeowner struggling to pay the mortgage. He somehow made it every month, but it was always a close call. At the very least, the small house didn't seem too big for one person. If they had bought a bigger house with the intention of starting a family, only to be divorced a year later, that would've been a bigger sting.

Not that that was any consolation.

When Eddie put his weight on the bottom step of the porch, he heard the familiar sound of the wood squeaking. He sighed, telling himself that he'd have to fix that sometime. It was the same thing he'd been telling himself since he and Judy had first looked at the house.

The problem was, Eddie knew it was a simple fix. The board was too loose. The screws holding it in place were rusty from being in the elements year-after-year. But the idea of doing yet another job after a long day's work was impossible. And the weekend? Forget it. He needed the full two days to recharge.

Inside, Eddie tossed his keys on the kitchen table, set his lunch box on top of the fridge, and went to the sink to wash his hands. It was the same routine he had every day. His hands were always filthy from everything he had needed to get into throughout the day.

As he dried them, the stillness of the empty house nearly swallowed him up. He went to the thermostat and turned up the heat a little, just to hear the furnace running to drown out the silence. He considered the radio, but the last thing he needed was to be screamed at by the hair bands. And talk radio with their annoying DJs and endless commercials was not anything he'd ever consider putting on himself.

He went to his bedroom and changed his clothes into something cleaner—and more comfortable—then took a seat in his usual chair in the living room. He reached for the newspaper that lay on the floor beside his chair and tried to get into the front page story.

The only thing he could hear was the ringing in his ears from the silence. The thought of the cold beer in the fridge haunted him. He needed to stop drinking, or else he'd end up a drunk like his father had been. Just because Eddie was divorced didn't mean he needed to continue the cycle of alcoholism that had been in his family for years.

Giving up on the paper, Eddie tossed it aside and rose

from his chair. The damn board on the front step would at least be a distraction. It would give him something to do before he had to make himself a measly dinner and go to sleep for the night. Yet another mundane routine he performed day-in and day-out.

In the basement, he gathered the tools he needed, then went out the front door and got to work on the step.

He tried the electric screwdriver, but the rusted nail broke before he could get it out far enough. Reaching for the crowbar, he pried the step up, relieving the tension and stress in his shoulders from the physical exertion.

The board came off cleanly. Eddie grabbed his hammer and was about to pound out the rest of the rusted nails, but stopped when he noticed a folded piece of paper tucked into the space beneath the board.

The page had yellowed with age. Dirt stains and water marks spotted the paper from the rain and the snow, but it was still intact.

Carefully, Eddie lifted it and unfolded the piece of paper. There was a handwritten letter that was dated October 17, 1924. Almost sixty years ago to the day.

What was most alarming, however, was that the letter was signed by a man who Eddie knew. The very same realtor who had sold him the house.

Frankie Walker.

More by the Author

To find more books by the author, visit
DavidNethBooks.com/Books

* * *

Subscribe to his newsletter to be the first to know of new
releases and special deals!
DavidNethBooks.com/Newsletter

* * *

**If you enjoyed the book, please consider leaving a
review on Goodreads or the retailer you bought it from.**
Reviews help potential readers determine whether
they'll enjoy a book, so any comments on what you
thought of the story would be very helpful!

About the Author

David Neth is the author of the Lost by Magic series, the Coven series, the Under the Moon series, the Heat series, the Fuse series, and other stories. He lives in Batavia, NY, where he dreams of opening his own bookstore.

Also writes small town romance as D. Allen.

www.DavidNethBooks.com
www.facebook.com/DavidNethBooks